LONE WOLF

THE TEXAS BRAND: GENERATIONS
BOOK FOUR

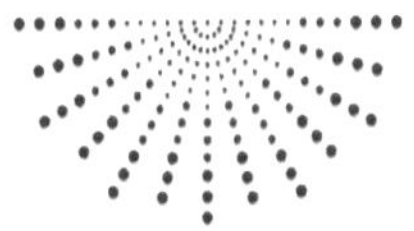

MAGGIE SHAYNE

CHAPTER ONE

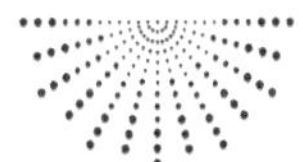

*H*is mother was dying and she was only forty-four. She looked far older though, ravaged by cancer. She wasn't going to recover and get out of the hospital. Not this time. And her nurses had told him it was close, so he'd stopped going in to work at all this week. He came in the morning, took a break at midday when she was usually sleeping, then headed back for the evening visiting hours.

He sat by her bedside and held her hand. She opened her eyes and looked into his, her gaze direct and clear. He hadn't seen that in a while. She said, "I'm too weak…to talk as much…as I should."

"You don't have to talk, Ma. I can do all the talking." He leaned over, holding her hand. Her copper-red curls had faded to the shade of ground ginger, and the roses had fled her cheeks.

"I thought I'd have…more time."

"I did too, Mom. A lot more."

She smiled at him, but it was weak, and her poor lips were so chapped it probably hurt. He quickly grabbed the lip balm from her bedside stand and went to put it on, but she held up a hand, bending her eyebrows. "No. Listen."

He lowered his hand, startled. Cilla had never snapped at him like that.

She took a breath, like getting mad had taken it out of her. Her eyes drooped, but she popped them open again. "You'll have to read the journals, I guess."

"What?"

"Too weak," she said, her voice becoming a whisper. "But you need to know."

"I need to know what?"

She muttered, "loose board" and "linen closet" before falling asleep.

He could tell she was down for the time being, so he kissed her forehead, tucked her blankets around her, uncovered her feet the way she liked, and then he went home, sure to his bones there would be no loose boards or hidden diaries to find in the linen closet. Morphine and dying did odd things to people. She said a lot of crazy things in the increasingly rare moments when she was awake.

And yet an hour later, he was standing in front of the linen closet on the second floor of their small, simple house. A section of paneling was leaning on the open closet door. Its shelves were on the hallway floor, towels and sheets and all, still folded. He'd moved them with care. No point making a mess.

He didn't even know his mother had *kept* journals. And why the hell would she hide them so thoroughly?

He was surprised when he found two small books behind the wall panel and took them both out. The top one's cardboard covers were wrapped in peeling red fake leather. The second one was yellow with daisies. He untied the first diary's pink ribbon and opened the small book. The date inside was only a few weeks older than he was.

Then he looked at his watch. He had to grab a sandwich, then help his boss for just a few hours. He could still make it back for late visiting hours with his mom.

He took the little red book with him to read later, by his mother's bedside during her intermittent naps.

Cilla Travail

August 10

I had a Greek mythology book in my backpack and seventy-five dollars in the pocket of my jeans-jacket when I rode my bike home from babysitting for the Belmonts today. It was seven p.m.

I used to keep my babysitting money in my music box. It was white with a ballerina inside, and it played Beethoven's "Fur Elise," cause I like the music so much. Stepdaddydearest keeps borrowing my babysitting money. Always promises to pay me back double, but he never pays me back at all.

Last time he asked, I told him I already spent it. Man, he lost his mind. Trashed my room, broke the lid off my jewelry box, and found the money. Then he backhanded me for lying and lectured me for an hour about being a selfish little brat who didn't want to help my family.

So this time I kept my cash on me, like I do this diary. It didn't matter though. Cause when I pedaled into my driveway, Mom's car wasn't there. I never like being home alone with my old man. He's always groping me when nobody else is around. Been doing that shit since I was eleven. Hands on my boobs, hands on my butt, hands on my crotch. It's worse when he puts his hands inside my pants, because then it hurts. Sometimes he just pulls me close and presses himself against me and breathes his stupid cigarette breath all over me. It's gross and I hate it, but he says he'll kill me if I tell, and that mom will never believe me anyway and hate me forever.

That part scares me most. That my mom will hate me. I feel so guilty for what he does to me that I bet it's probably true. She will hate me if she ever knows.

Mostly I just avoid him and pretend my life is normal. But I know better. I am not normal. When I'm around other kids my age, I feel like a freak, as if everyone can see it. I'm not the same as them. I don't fit in. I'm...weird.

So I got to the edge of our driveway, balanced the bike with one foot on the ground, about to pedal off and stay away until Mom got back, when Dad opened the front door and asked me why I was standing out there like an idiot, loud enough for every neighbor to hear.

I told him I was going to Shelly's, but that didn't work. He ordered me inside and asked if I got paid. I tried out my lie and it worked. He let the door bang closed and went back in.

I got off the bike, rolled it out of the driveway onto the grass, and walked inside about as slow as I could. When I got in though, he wasn't there waiting to grope me. He went straight to the family room in back where he spent most of his free time in his reclining chair with the window open, winter or summer, smoking cigarettes and watching television.

A vehicle pulled in and I sighed in relief. I thought Mom was home. He never touched me when Mom was home—except in the middle of the night, sometimes.

I was expecting Mom to walk in all smiles and rosy cheeks and clue-lessness, but instead, someone on the other side knocked.

So I opened the door.

Two men stood there, white guys. They didn't say anything for a second, but they looked at me in a way that felt weird. And then they looked at each other and grinned, and I got chills and didn't know why.

They asked if my dad was home, said he was expecting them. But before I could point the way, stepdaddydearest bellowed, "Back here, guys. You too, Priscilla.

I don't know how to explain this in words, but it was like my feet were glued to the floor. I felt like I was gonna throw up. The men started back, but I stayed where I was with my hand on the still-open door. I couldn't seem to close it. There was something bubbling, something like, Get out of here. Get out of here right now, *but I couldn't figure out why. I couldn't ignore it, though. I didn't really even think about it until later, when I had the time, finally, to sit still and write all this down. It was just like...I had to leave. I couldn't not leave. It was weird like that.*

I looked around, feeling panic bubble up for no reason. And I noticed the rack beside the wood stove with only two logs in it, and I said loudly that Dad would kick my ass if I didn't get some firewood in here.

Then I was out the front door. I didn't go to the woodpile but straight past it to my bike. I almost took off right then. But I was still arguing with myself for this sudden urge to piss off my old man in a way that was bound to have consequences I wouldn't like. And I was curious, I guess.

Miz O'Connor, my English teacher, says I have an inquisitive mind. My French teacher wants to send me to France next year as a foreign exchange student, but all Mom said when I told her was that the school must think parents are made of money and then asked what the hell I'd do in France.

Dad said what Dad always says. "No."

I hate him so much.

I pushed my bike around behind the house to that always-open window and laid it down real quiet in in the grass, then I went closer but stayed down low out of sight, and I listened.

One of the strangers asked how old I was, and Dad said fourteen, and then the other guy asked if I was a virgin. Dad said, "Fuck if I know," and the stranger said a number. Two thousand.

I gasped, then clapped my hand over my mouth and froze—I was so sure they'd heard me in there.

Dad haggled, asked for five, and said he was gonna have to go to all the trouble of convincing Mom I ran away, and that alone was worth five. And the other guy said he couldn't go higher than four and Dad said okay.

My blood felt like it had frozen. I shivered, but besides that, I was paralyzed.

Dad bellowed for me to get my ass in there, and I finally managed to move again.

I grabbed my bike and pedaled through the next three backyards fast as I could. I felt like I was being chased the whole time. I couldn't stop shivering, but I wasn't cold.

I veered into the little woodlot with the shortcut path everyone always takes to school. But I didn't stop at school either. I just kept pedaling and thinking my stepdad had just tried to sell me. To sell me! I don't even know what for. But I had to get away, as far away as I could go. I knew that for sure. Mom would never believe me if I told her. Nobody would.

After an hour of pedaling, I'd made it to the truck stop out near the highway exit. I don't know how many miles from home, but a ways. There were lots of rigs, big and small, filling the parking lot, coming and going non-stop. The smells coming from the deep fryer pulled me in that direction and my stomach growled. I had enough money to eat, but I was still too close to home to be seen or to even stop riding. Or at least to stop for very long. My old man would be out looking for me. So would Mom.

Poor Mom.

I pedaled into the parking lot. I didn't think I could ride my bike on the highway without getting caught, once everyone was out looking for me, and I had no idea where I was going. I wanted a map. And some of those fries that smelled so darn good.

But I didn't get either. I came upon a small truck with a bed full of cargo entirely covered by a blue tarp. The truck had Texas plates. I was in Binghamton, New York. Texas seemed like it would be far enough.

It was dark, and the closest parking lot light was busted out. So I got off my bike, rolled it closer, and took a look underneath the tarp. Just boxes, mostly cardboard, some wooden, all sealed. "Murray Sporting Goods" was stamped on some of them, and there was room in between. Two men were walking out of the diner, heading for their rigs. Another handful had just arrived, and the sound of big rig air brakes gusted as another one pulled in, his headlights spilling over me.

I crouched and pretended to fiddle with my bike chain until the parking lot was quiet again. Then I picked up my bike and shoved it underneath the tarp. I climbed in behind it, my heart pounding so hard I could hear it. I pulled the tarp back down and found a more or less comfortable spot to curl up and wait, then tried to move some of the boxes in front of me in case the driver looked. I couldn't hide the bike, though.

It didn't take long before I heard the truck's door open and felt it sink with the driver's weight as he got in. The door slammed, the engine cranked, and a few minutes later, the truck was pulling out onto the highway and picking up speed. And I got my diary out of my backpack, so I could write all this down.

My life kind of ended tonight, I think.

Priscilla Marie Bishop is dead.

From now on I'm Cilla Travail, born in the back of a truck in Broome County, New York, fully grown at fourteen and three-quarters years old.

WOLF

Wolf sucked in a breath, looking up from the journal at his mother in the hospital bed. She'd slept through his entire evening visit this time, but now he had questions.

"Ma," he said, leaning over the bed so his dark hair fell forward and touched her face. "I need you to wake up. Visiting hours are almost over."

He'd been shocked to his bones—realizing that he'd never even known his mother's real name.

Nor, apparently, his own.

"What the hell, Ma? What the *hell*?"

There came three gentle taps on the door. That was Kate, one of his mom's nurses. She didn't even bother sticking her head in anymore, just tapped three times to tell him time was up.

He closed his mother's diary, straightened, and turned around to pick up his backpack from the reclining chair Nurse Mindy had brought in for him. He'd come to believe over the past seventeen days that nurses were the best human beings on the planet. He didn't even mind that they made him leave when visiting hours ended every night. He was pretty sure they enforced the rules more for his sake than theirs.

He glanced at the clock on the wall, a round black one with a white face. 8:57. His mother, or rather her diary, had just dropped the bombshell of a lifetime on him, and now there was a forced intermission before he could learn anything else—if there was even anything else in the diary to learn.

He leaned down to kiss her cheek, as he did every night.

His mom was pale. She'd always been pale, but now she was white and her face was thin and drawn. She was only forty-four, fourteen years older than he was. The cancer had aged her so much you'd never know.

He'd put a recent photo of her on the bulletin board—skin like Irish cream, freckles scattered across her nose and cheeks, orange-red curls framing her face.

Even her hair was losing its color. She was fading before his eyes like a watercolor in the rain.

And he'd never even known her real name. He knew the rest —that she'd been a runaway teen when he was born, that she'd raised him with help from Grandma Sage. It had been just the three of them for as long as he could remember, until Grandma had died in her sleep without warning or fuss twelve years ago, and just the two of them ever since.

"Priscilla Maria Bishop," he whispered. And he covered her papery, frail hand with his brown one. "I love you, Ma."

She didn't respond. She'd been sleeping all afternoon. The nurses had warned him she'd start sleeping more, waking less, until eventually she wouldn't wake at all.

Straightening, he slid the strap of his canvas bag up over his shoulder, tucked the diary inside, rubbed the small of his back with his free hand, and walked quietly out of the room. He waved to Mindy and Kate at the nurses' desk, and they returned sad smiles that tried to convey comfort.

And then he headed out to his 1977 Ford truck. The front was still the original light blue, but it had faded to powder-with-rust. He turned the key to crank her up. She coughed a few times, but she started, and he patted the dash and said, "'Atta girl."

Snowflakes filled his headlight beams all the way back to their simple house in Hobbsville, about fifteen miles north of Borger, Texas, almost to the Oklahoma panhandle. They got a few inches every winter, but it always came as a surprise all the same. It was only November.

His head was full of questions. If his mother's name wasn't Travail, then neither was his. Was he a Bishop, then?

What about her piece-of-shit stepfather? Was he still around?

He stepped through the front door and looked around the house they'd shared for more than a decade. They'd moved around constantly when he was growing up, and he'd changed schools at least once a year. But once he'd landed a job on a union construction crew, they'd been able to buy a place of their own, a fixer-upper.

His truck was a fixer-upper too.

Hell, so was his *life*.

He wanted answers. And pouring through his mother's journals didn't seem likely to give those answers fast enough. So he went to her bedroom.

When he opened the door, he realized he hadn't been in there since the night he'd taken her to the ER. She hadn't told him she was terminal. That job had fallen to a stranger, a doctor who knew more about his mother than he did.

It turned out keeping secrets had been a way of life for her, hadn't it?

Her bed was unmade, just the way it had been when he'd

scooped her out of it, taking the blanket with them, wrapping her up along the way to the truck. He looked around, wondering where her secrets might be hidden—besides the diaries, which would take days to read.

Not many options for hiding places in the bedroom. It had been a den, but when she got too weak for the stairs, they'd made it her bedroom. Then later, they'd added the hospital bed, and later the commode and the IV pole. The whole time he'd been expecting her to recover, and wondering why it was taking so long.

He searched under the bed, inside the drawers of her dresser, the nightstand, and the closet. He checked the insides and bottoms of drawers and under the mattress. He felt for loose floorboards and false doors in the walls. He was wondering whether to slice open the mattress when someone knocked at his front door.

The intrusion startled him. When someone came around unexpectedly, it made him nervous. He'd never thought too much about that, but now that he was questioning everything about himself, he realized he'd been raised to be suspicious of strangers by a woman who had something to hide.

Two women, as Grandma Sage had always been tight-lipped about her past as well. Now that he thought about it, she probably wasn't related either.

What a trio they must've made, a green-eyed redhead, a black senior citizen, and a Native American kid without a clue.

He left the room, went to the door, opened it.

A woman stood there with a massive bundle of hair piled atop her lowered head in shades that shifted from caramel to blood-amber. Snow was falling behind her as she lifted her head, but her eyes were slower and took their time sliding up his body. By the time they locked onto his, her eyebrows were high.

"I…you…I…" She closed her lips, cleared her throat, but never let go of his eyes.

Hers were the darkest blue he'd ever seen. For a second, he forgot to breathe. Then she said his name and broke the spell. "I'm uh…looking for Wolf Travail."

"Not looking for him, looking *at* him."

"You're…Cilla Travail's son?"

"So I've been told." He was proud of himself for not missing a beat.

"Yeah. Okay. So, I'm Camellia Rio and I—"

"Camellia Rio? Really?"

She crooked one eyebrow and her chin rose.

He saw he'd offended her and spoke fast. "Sounds too pretty to be a real name is all."

"Like Wolf Travail, you mean?"

He had to lower his eyes fast. She was too quick for him, and he was sure it had flashed in his eyes—the knowledge that his name was made up. Probably. Not knowing was killing him.

"So full disclosure," she said. "I work for a lawyer."

"If it's about the hospital bills, I—"

"No, not about the bills. I agreed to help your mother. She had a small life insurance policy and she left instructions for—listen, can I come in? It's cold out here."

He turned to look at the house behind him. His mom's bedroom door was open, the mess he'd made going through her things fully visible. When he looked back at Camellia Rio, her blue eyes told him she'd already seen it. Snowflakes were gathering atop her mountain of hair. He sighed in surrender.

"Yeah, sure, come on in."

WILLOW BRAND, SKY DANCER RANCH, QUINN, TEXAS

At the family meeting she'd called, Willow yanked the sheet off the cradle in the middle of her mom's living room. The one with the name "WOLF" carved into it. She'd found it in the attic while her folks had been traveling, and she'd kept it to herself for as long as she could stand. Her anger had only grown. So she whipped off the sheet and let it sail to the floor in the corner with all due dramatic flair.

There was a collective gasp and Willow said, "What is this, Mom?"

Beside her, Jeremiah tightened his arm around her shoulders and whispered, "I thought you were gonna ease into it, babe."

She ignored him and continued. "We were looking in the attic for my old cradle for Lily and Ethan's baby, and we found this. What does this mean? Who's Wolf?"

Taylor, her mother, did not speak. She had gone still, staring at the cradle, her long black hair, streaked in silver, formed a smooth curtain over her face. But then she looked up and her brown eyes shifted to Willow, who was her younger mirror in every way.

"I—" Her beautiful face crumpled and she ran from the room with Willow's father, Wes, right on her heels.

"What the hell is going on?" Willow called after her parents as they ran outdoors, leaving the rest of the whole dang clan behind them.

A heavy hand fell on her shoulder—Uncle Garrett's hand. "I s'pose this talk is overdue." Then he looked around the room at the gathered Brands. All of the elders, their wives too, except Wes and Taylor. Aunt Chelsea was walking around with a pot, refilling coffee mugs. Willow's cousin and best friend Ethan moved closer to her side while his beautiful Lily's blue eyes beamed with concern, her hand resting atop her swollen belly.

Maria-Michelle and her new husband, Harrison, drew nearer. Cousins Trevor and Orrin leaned on either end of the mantel like opposite bookends, one as dark as the other was light, and Orrin's kid sister, Drew, blond and blue-eyed like her brother, sat on the hearthstone. Except for his black-framed eyeglasses and bigger build, Baxter could've been their older brother, with his shaggy golden mane.

As Willow looked from the stunned faces of the younger Brands to the expressions of their parents, resolved and expectant, it was clear most of the elders already knew whatever it was Uncle Garrett was about to say. Uncle Ben and Aunt Penny were not holding her gaze, but averting theirs whenever she looked their way.

Garrett moved to the center of the room and took a breath. Aunt Chelsea met his eyes and nodded, and he seemed to take courage from it. "Willow, sweetie, you were not your parents' firstborn child," he began.

Every one of Willow's cousins sent a wide-eyed look her way. And then Uncle Garrett told the story.

CHAPTER TWO

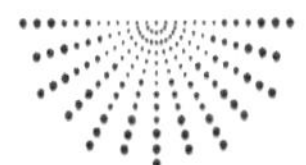

CAMELLIA RIO

Camellia knew that the woman calling herself Cilla Travail was a ginger-haired beauty with a soft smattering of freckles across her nose and that her real name was Priscilla Bishop.

She hadn't expected Cilla's "son" to look like heaven in blue jeans, with long black hair that made her fingers want to touch it, and brown eyes full of pain and confusion. He was so beautiful that for a moment she'd forgotten her own name. He was Native American, not red Irish like Priscilla.

Not that she'd expected him to look like her.

The house was small and neat, except for that one room. While not trashed, she could see that it had clearly been searched. Funny, though, how the stacks of clothing on the hospital-style bed were still folded, placed specifically enough that she thought they were in order, and the things on hangers were draped across the bottom. Drawers were open and empty. The cushion was off the rocking chair, but standing upright against it.

Cilla's room had been searched.

Neatly.

Wolf waved her to the living room where a braided oval rug lay beneath a floral-patterned camelback sofa and a matching loveseat with pretty wood trim. Some clothes lay on one cushion and her host scooped them up—a button-down flannel shirt and a T-shirt, she thought.

Cilla said he worked on a construction crew. The image of him coming in at the end of a hard day, peeling off his shirts on his way to a hot shower, popped in unbidden. She traced his imaginary path with her eyes and, sure enough, there was a closed door at the end of it. Bathroom, for sure.

She should not be this attracted to him. This job could be a threat to her recent vow of celibacy and aspirations to old maid-hood.

"Have a seat," he said. "You want anything? And by anything, I mean a coffee or a beer, and it's kinda late for coffee."

"Is the beer cold?" She sat down on the cute sofa. There was an old-fashioned look to the place, coffee table and end tables like her own mom's, with little doilies on them and stacks of coasters. There was a TV mounted to the wall.

He must know, she thought. Why else go through his mother's room like that unless he was looking for the truth?

Was he angry?

Was he dangerous?

A ripple of apprehension tiptoed over her spine and she looked at the room again. Nothing had been thrown or broken. It looked like a careful, respectful search, not a temper tantrum.

Her spine relaxed slightly.

Wolf Travail headed deeper into the house, and when he flipped on the lights, she could see all the way into the kitchen where he'd gone. In seconds, he was heading toward her again with two dewy brown longnecks. He opened them both, then handed her one and took the rocking chair between the sofa and loveseat.

He moved with an easy grace that didn't go with the strain on his face.

His *really* handsome face.

"So Ma has life insurance? You know she's still alive, right?"

"Yeah. I know. She left word with her doctor to call her lawyer when she'd passed, or was near passing, if it could be known, and he let me know. I'm so sorry you're losing your mother right now. I can't even imagine."

Her voice cracked at the end, and that seemed to make him look at her. She was embarrassed that her eyes burned, but the thought of losing her mom... She reached across to put a hand over his, where it rested on the arm of the chair. "I'm deeply sorry. I mean it."

"Thank you," he said, and he was looking into her eyes like he could see that she meant it. "You're the first person to say that to me, besides her nurses."

She felt for him. Especially because she was about to tell him that he wasn't who he thought he was—that none of the things he thought he knew about himself were true. She took a drink of the beer, ice cold and perfect. "So...you were looking for something?" As she asked, she nodded toward the bedroom.

He glanced that way, too. "Yeah. It's uh...personal."

Yeah, he wasn't going to admit anything, even if he knew. And why should he? He didn't know who she was or why she'd come.

She guessed she might as well just spit it out, then.

She took a breath, then said, "Travail wasn't your mom's real name. She's been using Cilla Travail ever since she left home at fourteen."

He leaned forward suddenly. "How do you know that?"

"She told me."

He still seemed confused, but he was studying her face like the answers he needed might be found there. "Do you know...?"

Then he paused and searched the room as if for the right question. No wonder. He probably had a thousand. "...where I was born?" he asked at length.

Her heart clenched at how eagerly he asked it. She spoke slowly, carefully. "The official records say it was a home birth, attended by a midwife who's since died. Your birth certificate was issued as Wolf Travail. Cilla didn't change her own name legally until much later."

"Probably couldn't afford it." He took a deep breath, closed his eyes as if to gather his thoughts. When he opened them again though, the tension lines between his eyebrows had remained. "I still don't understand why you know these things."

"Cilla's lawyer asked me to look into things to make sure none of this messed up the insurance payout. It's only twenty-five thousand, but—"

"*Dollars?*"

"Yes. The lawyer helped her apply for Medicaid. It was just approved. She might not even know yet. But you won't have to worry about that. Anything not covered can go onto a payment plan."

"How the hell did she do all that?"

"He says she paid a little from her paychecks every week, but uh..." She shrugged. "But I think they might've had a thing once. Just a vibe I get."

He nodded. "Makes sense. Men fall for my Mom, always have, but as soon as they start getting too close, she cuts 'em loose." He sighed deeply, his grief in his eyes. Then he said, "And how do you fit into all this?"

"Well, the lawyer hired a private investigator on your mom's behalf—me."

"You're an investigator."

She nodded. "I was paid in advance to...help you figure things out."

His brown eyes were swimming in emotion. "Like what things?" he asked.

"Like...who you are." She'd said too much. She was trying to ease into this for his sake. She felt for him. It was way too easy to do.

Wolf looked at her for a long moment. He took a thoughtful pull from his beer, then set it on the stand. "That doesn't make a lot of sense, Camellia. If my mother wanted me to know the truth, why not just tell it to the lawyer?" He looked up at the ceiling, shaking his head so his long black hair moved behind him. "Why would she make it so complicated? Why would she need a PI when she could've just told me herself?"

"She couldn't just tell you herself because she's never known."

He frowned hard, rising from his chair. It kept rocking after he stood. "What does that even mean?"

She rose, too, gauging the distance to the door before she went on. "When Cilla was fourteen years old, Wolf, she found you washed up along the banks of the Rio Grande after a flash flood had raged miles upstream. She mistook you for an immigrant baby and was afraid of what would happen to you if she turned you over to the authorities. So she just...kept you."

His eyes were as wide as the universe just then, and the pain that swirled in them just as infinite. There was no anger, no menace there. He didn't smash anything or swear or punch a wall. She didn't think he was that kind.

Not like Earl.

WOLF

The room started spinning and not from the beer. Wolf reached out for balance and clasped the woman's shoulder. He hadn't meant to, but before he could pull his hand away, she covered it with one of hers, and said, "I know this is a shock."

His mouth was open, but he wasn't breathing. He was looking inward, focused on nothing. And what he found inside himself was hollow. His mother had *found* him? Who the hell *was* he?

Camellia brought her beer bottle around and pressed it to the back of his neck. He sucked in a sharp breath at the chilly contact, then met her eyes. "She *found* me?"

"Yeah. She did. And this." She pulled a wad of brown paper from the pocket of her flannel-lined denim jacket, ducking away as she did, so his hand fell from her shoulder to his side again. She handed it to him.

He took the packet and shivered all the way to his bones as he unwrapped it to find a small leather bracelet that spelled out his name in beads: "WOLF." The O was a round moonstone bead with a howling wolf's head carved into it.

"Cilla told me this was tied around your wrist when she found you."

He looked up again. Her dark blue eyes were wet.

"I've been paid in advance to help you find out where you came from, Wolf—if and when that's something you want to do. Okay?"

"I—I don't know. I can't even think right now."

"I wouldn't ask you to decide anything now," she said quickly. "Look, I met with your mom and Dan Tyner—the attorney—a couple of times when she was setting all this up. Her story... It got to me, that's all. I'm at your disposal, okay? Whenever you're ready."

He peeled apart the curtain of confusion for a moment. She was taking a card from a pocket, handing it to him. "At least you know your name is really Wolf. At least, that's what the bracelet suggests."

He said, "If you talked to Ma, you probably know more about me than I do."

"It's all in the diaries. She told me it was. But I'll tell you anything you want to know. Anything I know, at least."

He nodded. "I was…searching her bedroom for answers. Easier ones, faster ones, I guess."

She nodded. "I'd like to…visit her, if that would be okay with you. I want to let her know that her wishes are being carried out. It was important to her. All she had to leave you, she said."

"Sure, but…there's not much time." His throat convulsed so hard it hurt. He tried to swallow, failed, and when he spoke again, his voice was strained. "You want to meet me at the hospital in the morning? I usually get some breakfast at the diner around the block before visiting hours start."

"Wow. Every day, huh?"

"This week. The last two I went after my shift at work."

"You're a good son."

"Yeah, but whose?" He lowered his head, shaking it slowly. "Sorry. I promise I won't wallow in self-pity for more than a few hours. I'm just…still reeling. I don't even know what questions to ask you."

"Don't ask me anything. Let me tell you everything she told Dan and me. In the morning, over breakfast. And in the meantime, you've got journals to go through. What time? In the morning?"

"Eight a.m. too early?"

"Eight's good," she said. "See you then. Or, if you need me sooner…" She didn't finish the sentence, just nodded at the card she'd set on the coffee table's doily, gathered the lined hood of her jacket up around her ears, and headed out into the gently falling snow.

WILLOW BRAND, SKY DANCER RANCH

"He was perfect in every way," Uncle Garrett said in his low, deep voice.

Willow was dying to hear the story of her brother, but she was also worried about her mom. She'd never seen her look the way she'd looked when Willow had uncovered the cradle.

"His name was Jonathon Wolf Brand," Garrett went on. "Johnny Wolf, we called him. He was born on September first, just two years before you, Willow."

Her throat tightened painfully and her eyes burned. "I had a brother."

Aunt Chelsea came closer and hugged her, but that meant Jeremiah had to let go. "He was gone before you came along, honey," she said.

"Flash flood came through that year," Garrett went on. "Your mamma, she was on her way to the clinic, taking Wolf for his first checkup. He was just two weeks old. The water came on like a demon. No warning. It just came. It took the car, smashed it into a tree. She got him out of the back as it filled with water, but then another wave came and swept 'em both right out into the river. She tried to hold onto him. She *fought* to hold onto him. But the current took that baby right out of your mamma's arms."

"Ohmygod," Willow whispered as her cousins closed ·ranks around her.

Ethan, the eldest, asked, "How could you not tell us this, Dad?"

It was his mom, Chelsea, who spoke up, though, not Garrett. She said, "Taylor couldn't get over it. I don't know how anyone could. She…had what they used to call a nervous breakdown and wound up spending six months in-patient in a psychiatric hospital."

Willow's throat spasmed and made her gulp aloud.

"We never found his little body," Garrett said, and his voice broke on the words. "Every police department up and down the border was looking for him, too, but...discreetly. If it'd hit the press, it would've done Taylor in." He lowered his head slowly. "I had the power to keep it kinda quiet."

"We held a memorial," Uncle Ben said. "But Wes didn't want a marker. He thought it would be too much for your mother, and he didn't want to lose her again." Ben hugged his wife Penny a little closer. He'd lost her once, long ago, so he knew the pain of that.

"We just never talked about little Johnny Wolf after that," Uncle Elliot said. It was clear the way he was looking at Aunt Esmeralda that she was hearing this for the first time, too. "It was easier that way, and pretty soon all of us fell into silence about him."

"It was never meant to be a family secret," Uncle Adam added. "It just became one."

"I think that's how all family secrets work," Ethan's bride, Lily, said softly.

Maria-Michelle was shaking her head at her mom and dad, Jessie and Lash. "I can't believe this. And nobody ever found him?"

Drew, the youngest, smallest, and blondest cousin, rose from her spot on the hearth and looked around the room. Her hair was in a high-riding ponytail that whipped so hard when she turned her head that it should've had a sound-effect. "How's everybody so sure he's dead, then?"

"Because a newborn rescued from floodwaters would've made the news, hon," her mom, Penny, said.

"Yeah, and so would a dead baby pulled from the floodwaters, wouldn't it?" Drew shot back. "But there wasn't one. Was there?"

The elder Brands shook their heads, exchanging worried looks.

"What if he floated to shore across the border?" Drew went on. "No, no, people, I'm sorry, but if there's no body, there's no proof of death. No way." She surged toward the front door like her feet were on fire but stopped and turned. "Willow, you okay?"

"Of course she's not okay," Maria-Michelle said, pulling Willow right out of Jeremiah's arms. "We're taking her home. Lily? Drew?"

Drew glanced almost desperately at her brother. Orrin, reading her mind, nodded so subtly that nobody else noticed. But Willow noticed. Her aspiring sleuth cousins, Drew and Orrin, were planning something.

"I think I'd better go after my mom," Willow said. Then she looked at the cradle, and regret swamped her as she realized she'd just stuck a knife into her mother's broken heart. "Somebody please put that thing back in the attic."

CAMELLIA RIO

Camellia went home to the cute little Cape Cod in Hobbsville, Texas, where she'd grown up. It was her mom's place, with a matching two-car garage and a vacant 2nd story apartment she did not want to have to rent. She was in between places now. She'd wanted to be with her mom after her dad had passed away unexpectedly. Heart attack a year ago.

She'd let her old apartment go, because Earl knew where it was, and God knew how many keys he'd had made. She just figured when her mom didn't need her anymore, she'd find a new place, maybe even in a new town. Though it would be tough to leave her mom all alone.

The house was white with dark green shutters, window boxes, and green roof shingles. When she opened the front door, the scent of roasting potatoes and herbs wrapped around her like a welcoming hug.

"Is that you, Camellia?" her mom called from the kitchen in exactly the same tone she called it every night.

"Yeah, Mom, it's me. Dinner smells great."

"New recipe. It's Monday, you know."

"Right, Meatless Monday." Her mom's latest awakening was underway. Erica Rio had one every three or four years. She liked to say she was in a constant state of evolution. She'd taken art classes, and there was a roomful of her watercolors to prove it. She'd taken belly dance classes and had the abs to prove that. Now she was inching her way into veganism a meal at a time.

When her only daughter had been born, Erica had been earning her certification in flower essence therapy. Hence the name. Camellias were peaceful, patient, accepting, and aligned with their true nature.

The name hadn't really taken, then, had it?

She was neither peaceful nor patient, and it had taken her twenty-six years to get aligned with her true nature as an independent, single woman. Her most recent and worst boyfriend of all time had shown her the light. Hallelujah, amen.

She dropped her keys into the bowl by the door and thought again about Wolf Travail. The poor guy, losing his mother and his identity all at the same time. The pain in his eyes had reached straight into her heart.

She went into the kitchen and hugged her tall, lean, quirky mother. For some reason, she felt tears threaten as she did. "I love you, Mom."

"I love you too, honey," she said, but softly, and then she turned, clasped her face, and stepped back to examine it. "You okay?"

Camellia shook her head. "Hard case today. How about you?"

"Better all the time. It's taken a year, but I think I've finally stopped waiting for life to go back to normal without your dad. Set the table, hon. The big bowls for this."

The topic switch gave her whiplash, but Camellia caught up,

grabbed the big bowls, plus spoons and napkins, and took them to the dining room table. Her mom followed with a large bowl of rice and another of roasted vegetables. "I'm settling into my *new* normal," she said. "It's not the same. It's different, and it will always be different. I've accepted that. But I'm going to make it as good as I can."

She sat down. Camellia covered her hand. "That's a huge step, Mom."

"Here's another one," she said. "I've been thinking about selling the house."

Camellia felt her face react but tried to hide her surprise and dismay. She had expected to inherit the house. And either live in it or sell it and explore new places. She was making decent money investigating for insurance companies and attorneys, but even then, mortgages were huge.

But that was not, she reminded herself, her mother's problem. So she wiped the disappointment off her face and nodded, and said, "I see."

"The property taxes, school taxes, and all the maintenance are more than rent would be in a nice apartment," her mother said. "And I'd be closer to people. I feel like I'm keeping you from living your life just because I don't want to be alone."

"I love being with you, Mom. And it's given me time to save some money, too, so I can have my own place someday."

"I know," her mom said. "If the house sells, I'll give you half. It's your inheritance, after all."

"That's really generous."

"Well, like I said, I'm only thinking about it." She sighed. "I'm also thinking about a new town. What do you think?"

"I've been feeling a little bit of wanderlust myself, Mom. I'd be open to a new town," she said. "It'd be an adventure."

Her mom smiled, clearly relieved. "I'll miss you on my cruise."

"I'll miss you too," she told her mom.

"So, tell me about your day. Is this the dying woman with the secret identity?"

Camellia wasn't supposed to discuss her cases, but she told her mother everything. It hurt no one and kept Erica from grieving so much. She'd do worse things to ease her mother's pain. "Yeah. I met the son tonight. He's…not what I expected."

"No?" Erica poured a little balsamic glaze over the veggies in her bowl, then reached across the table to offer her the bottle.

Camellia drizzled while Wolf Travail's brown eyes appeared in her mind. "No. I had to tell him. He was pretty upset."

"Poor man. What's he like?"

"He's the handsomest man I've ever seen in my life, Mom."

Her mother paused with the fork almost to her mouth.

"The kind of handsome that smacks you in the face, you know? When he opened the door, I just gaped for a second."

"*Oh?*"

"Don't say it like that. And yes, he's single."

"I didn't ask if he was single."

"It was in your 'oh'."

"When are you seeing him again?"

"We're having breakfast together, during which I'll probably tell him more stuff that'll ruin his life. And then I'm going to visit his dying mother. It's not a first date, trust me. Besides, this guy doesn't even know which end is up right now, and the last thing I need is another broken man-child to try fixing. Or any man, since I've sworn off them for good."

"He seems broken to you?"

"In the ten minutes I talked to him, you mean?"

"He's going through a rough patch, though," her mother said. She broke off a piece of bread, then gestured with it. "I bet I could tell in ten minutes."

Camellia sighed. "This is just a job. Understand?"

"Clearly," her mother said.

"I mean it, Mom. If you happen to meet this guy, you're gonna want it to be more. Hell, you'll want to adopt him. But it's not going to be like that. I really want you clear on it. Okay?"

"That pretty, is he?" She bit off another hunk of bread with a little growl, while smiling on one side.

Willow rolled her eyes, then said, "This meal is amazing." She dug in, because she was thinking about those brown eyes again. Wolf Travail was definitely going through a rough patch. Whatever else he was remained to be seen.

At three a.m., Camellia's cell phone buzzed repeatedly on the nightstand, and when she reached for it, she missed and knocked her water bottle to the floor. She got the phone on the second try, though, then blinked at its screen.

Text from an unknown number.

> Hospital called. My mother is close. If you want to see her, come now.

She pushed her hair out of her face, squinting at the bright screen, and tapped out a reply.

WOLF

The pickup started on the first try. After sitting for a few hours, it usually took at least three cranks, and on a night this chilly, four. But tonight, it felt like the old truck knew.

Wolf wished he'd stayed somewhere closer to the hospital. He should have. It was only thirty minutes, but he and the truck shaved a few minutes off that time. There was plenty of parking near the main entrance. A nurse he didn't know was waiting at the door and took him straight in, no ID check or sticky badge like usual. That told him things were dire.

When he arrived at his mom's door, someone was already

there at her bedside, holding her hand and speaking softly, her face hidden by a hank of honey-gold hair that had pulled free of its untidy pile.

Camellia Rio. She'd made it there before him.

"I'm doing what you asked, Cilla," she was saying to his ma. Her voice was soft but clear, and she was leaning in close, as if to make sure she could hear. "I'll help him all I can. He has the diaries, so he'll know everything you wanted him to know. And he's gonna be okay. I can tell." Her thumb moved in slow motion across the back of her frail hand, a soothing caress. "He's on his way. He'll be here any minute, okay?"

"I'm here now, Ma." He said it loud enough for her to hear as he stepped into the hospital room. Camellia lifted her head to look his way. Her cheeks were wet and her eyes were welling.

"He's here, Cilla. Wolf is here."

She backed out of the way as he moved up into her place beside the bed and covered his mom's hand with his own. But before he leaned down to kiss her, Camellia's hand fell on his shoulder, and her lips moved near his left ear. "I'll hang around awhile." And then she left the room, her footsteps soft on the floor.

Wolf looked at his mom, but she wasn't the person in the bed. He thought most of Cilla was already gone from her poor, ravaged body. Still, Camellia had spoken to her as if she could hear. And if she could hear him at all, he knew the words she'd be longing for.

"I'm right here, Ma. I'm holding your hand. I know the truth. I know you found me in the river and pulled me out and saved my life and then devoted your own to raising me."

Her eyes moved beneath their lids. The beeping of the machines picked up pace.

God, could she really hear him?

"It's okay," he said. "Everything's okay. And I'm gonna be okay, too, I promise."

Her eyes opened, green and clear and lucid and looking right into his.

"Thanks for pulling me out of the Rio Grande, Ma. I love you."

Her lips pulled into the shadow of a smile, then parted and whispered what sounded like "love." Then her pretty eyes closed, and Cilla Travail's short and difficult life ended.

CAMELLIA

Camellia hadn't made it all the way to the waiting room when the steady beeps of Cilla's monitor become a drone. Her heart lurched. She pivoted and ran back into the room just as Wolf straightened from his mother and turned toward the door, his face wet with tears.

She went in and hugged that man as hard as she'd ever hugged anyone in her life.

He didn't move for a moment, and then he did. His arms came around her, and his head bent low and his chest heaved.

She held him for a long time, until at length, he took a deep, steadying breath and loosened his grip.

"Come on," she said. "Come on with me."

He looked back at the hospital bed.

From behind Camellia, a nurse said, "Your mom's okay now, Wolf. You can go. We'll take care of her."

Nodding, Wolf turned to touch his mother's face one last time, and then he let Camellia take him home.

A short while later, Camellia stood beside her mother outside the guest room door. She'd texted ahead, so Mom had been ready with herbal tea and a gentle sedative. She'd been a nurse until she retired, and she always had good meds on hand. Wolf had accepted both with thanks, then crawled into bed with his clothes on. Thankfully, he'd fallen asleep almost as quickly.

As Camellia pulled the bedroom door closed, her mom said, "I thought you told me you were done bringing broken men home?"

Camellia paused, the door still open just a crack. "It's just for the night. And I don't think he's broken. Just bruised to hell and gone."

"Yeah," her mom replied. "I couldn't have left him there either."

"That sedative you gave him worked fast."

"He probably hadn't eaten. That poor man. That poor, sad, *gorgeous* man. You were *not* kidding about that."

"I hope he's gonna be okay," Camellia said, and she pulled the door closed. "I can't even imagine losing you, much less finding out the same day that you're not really Erica Rio and, moreover, that you didn't give birth to me, but plucked me out of a river with no idea where I came from. I think I'd be curled in a corner, sucking my thumb."

"No, you wouldn't. You'd do exactly what you're going to do for him. Beat the bushes till you scare out the truth."

"You're right," she said with a firm nod. "That's exactly what I'm going to do."

"Yes, you're gonna help that young man out. But in the meantime, you need to help yourself out, too. Are you gonna be okay with all this?

"I'm a professional," she said. "And a confirmed bachelor. I'll be fine."

"*Ooookay,*" said her mom. But she didn't sound like she believed it.

CHAPTER THREE

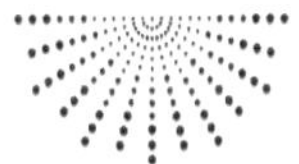

WOLF

olf woke up to a different world.

He was in a strange room with white curtains in a white bed covered with a fat white comforter. The walls were palest blue with a border of stenciled flowers near the ceiling. It was a feminine room, and for a moment he didn't know why he was in it. But then he remembered. His mom had died and Camellia Rio had brought him home to her own.

He was mildly embarrassed, and then worry crept in.

A soft tap came on his bedroom door, and when it opened, an older version of Camellia peered in at him. Her blue eyes were a shade lighter than her daughter's, and her hair was just as long, but its multiple shades went from silver to dark gray. He'd met her last night and struggled to recall her name.

She leaned in. "You're awake. Good. If you're groggy, it's a sedative hangover." When he raised his eyebrows in surprise, she said, "Don't worry. I'm a nurse. Retired now. That's why we live so near the hospital. I used to walk to work more often than not."

"That's why Camellia got there first, I guess." He closed his eyes, rubbed his head.

"Food will help, and I've got plenty."

"You've been too kind already, Mrs. Rio. I couldn't—"

"It's already cooking, so don't make a fuss. And it's Erica. I can bring it up here or—"

"I'll come down."

"Bathroom's down the hall, first door on the left." She pointed as she said it. "I left a change of clothes in there for you. My late husband's, and he'd be overjoyed to share them. They'll be too wide and too short, I reckon, but good enough to get you home."

"I should get back to the hospital." He blinked three times, unsure of why. "Shouldn't I?"

"No, hon. No need to go back there. I called and checked in, and she's already been moved to the funeral home."

The words hit. He felt the blow. His mother was at a funeral home. It didn't make sense to his mind. And then it made less. "But I didn't even pick one yet."

"Your mamma left her wishes with the staff. Apparently, she'd made her own arrangements."

Trying to take care of him. Even while she was dying, she was looking out for him.

"I'll see you downstairs when you're ready." She pointed again. "First door on the left," she reminded him.

So he followed directions, because it felt like the easiest thing to do and maybe the most he could manage at the moment. He showered, he dressed, he thought about how different his mother was from Camellia's. If he'd brought home a raggedy stranger, she'd have only greeted him at the front door to close it in his face. Cilla didn't trust strangers, nor abide them sniffing around, nor had Grandma Sage.

But there he was in the home of strangers on the day after the worst night of his life, sitting at a table with two women who did the things only women could do. They soothed and healed and comforted with their voices, with their eyes, with food, and that caring felt great, except for his underlying suspicion of ulterior motives.

Then again, he'd seen tears in Camellia's eyes at his mother's bedside, and when she'd held him, he'd felt her sadness even beyond his own.

In his experience, however, people were never this nice without a reason. He just didn't have the energy to know or care what it was. He ate the breakfast, which was delicious, thanked them for their kindness, and told them he had to go.

Camellia followed him to the door. "I'll give you a ride back to your truck."

"Hospital's within walking distance, your mom said."

She nodded. "About a fifteen-minute walk. I can give you directions."

He held up his phone, where a walking route to the hospital already filled the screen.

"Do you um…want to reschedule that talk? You really should have all the information."

He nodded. "Yeah, just…not now. Not yet."

"Okay," she said. "I get it." She lowered her head. "I'm really sorry about your mom," she said. "Be okay, okay?"

"I will. She'd kick my ass otherwise."

The door was open. No snow remained from the night before —it was too warm for that. It was a chilly, gray, wet morning. He held onto Camellia's eyes for a moment longer than felt casual. "I don't know how to thank you for…all this," he said.

And she said, "I do."

There it was. The ulterior motive, the reason for all the kindness. He knew there had to be one. "Really?"

She nodded. "Yeah. Let me help you find your birth family. I promised your mother. My mom knows that, because I don't have a lick of professional discretion where she's concerned. She'll never let me hear the end of it until I help you find them."

He was so surprised he couldn't think of an answer.

She said, "You have my number. Call me when you're ready, okay?"

He sort of nodded. She went back inside and closed the door. At the window to the left, her mother waved at him.

He didn't know how he felt about taking Camellia Rio up on her offer. He didn't feel the need to replace his dead family with a new one.

The only thing he felt sure about right then was that he wanted to lose himself in his mom for a little while, in her words, in those diaries. So after a detour to the funeral home—he got the info from the hospital—he headed home, got comfortable, and picked up where he'd left off in his mother's diaries, and in her life.

CILLA

Later, same day or maybe early the next

It's night now and we've been on the road for so many hours I've lost count. Twenty minutes ago, the driver finally made a stop—probably he had to pee as bad as I did. When I pulled back the tarp, I spotted a big neon sign across the entire roof of the place. "LUCKY'S TRUCK STOP —SHOWERS, MEALS, SUPPLIES!"

When I first got out, I couldn't tell where I was. The license plates on the vehicles in the parking lot came from like a dozen different states.

It was getting dark again. I didn't see any road signs, but I was pretty sure I was far enough from home to be safe and I had to pee so bad I could hardly move.

I went into the diner. A juke box was playing kind of low, and people sat in booths and in stools in front of a counter. I asked a wait-ress for a basket of fries, then headed for the restroom.

There was a whole shower room back there, and I could smell the soap and the steam. A shower would be nice, but I was afraid I wouldn't have enough time.

When I came back out of the restroom, I checked outside to be sure my ride was still there, and it was.

A pretty waitress handed me a big cardboard basket overflowing with French fries and a whole handful of ketchup packets. "I gave you extra," she said with a wink.

"Thanks." I said it on autopilot, taking the fries but paying no attention to the waitress. I wasn't sure which of the people at the counter was driving the truck I was riding in, and I skimmed their faces, trying to guess. The whole time I was in there, I was worried my ride would leave without me if I took too long. My bike was still in the truck, and I didn't want to lose it.

There was a payphone in there. I thought about calling my mom. But then I figured she'd see where I was calling from and send the cops to drag me back, and what if the next time my stepdad tried to sell me, I couldn't get away?

It's blowing my mind how something told me to get out of there. How did I know?

I bought a blanket and pillow in a cute little "travel bundle," plus two bottles of Coke, and a box of Hostess Twinkies. Then I took my fries in one hand, my bag of purchases in the other, and I went back to the truck with my haul.

So that was the whole deal. I'm back in, way more comfy with my blanket and pillow, eating my fries and trying not to leave grease stains on the pages as I write.

What was up with the people in the truck stop, though? There were men and women, travelers and waitresses. A few of them looked at me and it made me nervous, but nobody came up to me and asked if I was okay, or if I needed help. I was relieved, not to have anybody bugging me and maybe figuring out I was a runaway. But shouldn't they care? Shouldn't a 14-year-old alone in a truck stop in the middle of nowhere raise a few questions?

It seemed weird. I was so worried about getting caught and sent back, but instead, it kind of feels like I'm invisible.

Guess I'll put this down and read a while. I still have my Greek mythology book in my backpack. I'm afraid that's one book the library's never getting back. Maybe I'll mail it someday. After I read it a thousand more times.

I love mythology. In the stories, before she was a monster, Scylla was a princess who'd betrayed her father. My name is Cilla, and my father betrayed me.

WILLOW, SKY DANCER RANCH

"How's your mom?" Drew asked.

Willow's little, blond aspiring-private-eye cousin was standing in the doorway of Wes and Taylor Brand's home on Sky Dancer Ranch, looking worriedly past Willow, who'd answered her knock.

Willow nodded. "She's upstairs. Dad won't let me near her. Doc Elena's with her, giving her a sedative, Dad said. He said I should leave her alone for a while."

"*Jeeze.*"

"Yeah, he's really pissed." Sighing, Willow stepped back to let Drew inside, closed the door, and led her toward the kitchen. Her petite cousin glanced up the staircase when they passed, but Willow wanted to avoid seeing her father again at the moment. She felt guilty as hell.

"But your *mom?* In *bed?* With a *sedative?* She's one of the kick-assiest women in the family."

"I know."

"Next to you, I mean. You come by it honestly."

Willow heard her, but the words skated across the surface of her mind without leaving marks. She opened the fridge, took out a beer, and wished it was whiskey, then held it out to her cousin, but Drew shook her head. So she slammed the fridge door, twisted off the cap, tossed it toward the wastebasket, and missed. The cap hit the cabinet door, ricocheted across the floor, and spun on its end before falling with its pointy edges up.

"I can't believe they kept this from me. And they're acting like *I'm* the one who did something wrong." She could whine to her cousins. They were as close as any siblings, Willow thought. Then again, how would she even know what having a sibling felt like?

Drew shrugged one shoulder and averted her eyes.

"What? *You* think I did something wrong?" Willow asked, stunned.

"No!" Drew opened the fridge and took out a beer, apparently having changed her mind. She tossed her cap and it went into the wastebasket without touching the sides. Then she went over, picked up Willow's cap, and dropped it into the basket before taking a generous sip.

"You *do* think I did something wrong, don't you?" Willow was a deputy sheriff. She could tell when a suspect was stalling for time.

"I just think you could've been...gentler."

"I was pissed!"

"I don't blame you." Drew looked around. "So Jeremiah's not here?"

"He's helping out at the saloon today. No school today, so Frankie's at the house with Beans, which is his favorite place to be."

"Him and that dog..." Drew shook her head, smiling. "Frankie's staying at your place more and more, isn't he?"

Willow nodded. "Yeah. We, uh, brought up the notion of taking formal custody with his grandparents. That way they could go back to *being* grandparents."

"How did they respond?"

"Well…they didn't throw us out. And they didn't say no. They're talking to a lawyer and considering it."

"Aw, Willow, that's wonderful!"

"Yeah, it is." Willow smiled fully for the first time in quite a while. She'd been walking on air about her little family taking shape; her and Jeremiah and Frankie and his horse of a dog who'd brought them all together. Everything had been perfect until this bombshell had dropped right into the middle of the clan.

Footsteps made them look up. Elena Rodriguez, the newest member of the cousin-hood, and a doctor to boot, came down the stairs. She was one of four non-blood Brands. Ethan was adopted. Elena and Jeremiah were his half-siblings. Same Italian father, but different moms. Elena's mom was of Mexican descent, and the combination was stunning. She looked like Sophia Loren cranked up a notch, Willow and the other she-Brands had decided.

Elena wore jeans, boots, a pretty turquoise peasant blouse, had eyes like a woodland doe's and dark wavy hair. No white coat, but she was carrying a little black doctor's bag that could've come off the set of an old western.

"Hey," Elena said. "You okay, Willow?"

Willow was touched, but sick of being asked. Jeremiah had been asking it every time he looked at her since they'd found the cradle. And Drew, of course. Drew adored her.

She shrugged and said, "How can I be okay when I don't know what happened to my brother?"

"How can your mom be okay when she doesn't know what happened to her baby?" Elena asked the question gently, placing a hand on Willow's shoulder as she did.

Will figured it was the voice she reserved for dying patients and their bereaved families, or for delivering scary diagnoses at the clinic in Quinn. Her words didn't skim the surface of

Willow's brain like Drew's had. They stabbed straight through the ice into the depths. "Poor Mom. All this time, never knowing," she whispered.

"No wonder she never spoke about it," Drew said. "I mean, it's still the wrong call, but I can kind of understand it. Imagine her guilt—that she couldn't hold onto him. You know?"

"Even the strongest mind can break under pressure like that," Elena said. "Her history and files are at the clinic. It was before my time, but she consented to me looking at them. It was a serious breakdown, Willow."

"Are there unserious breakdowns?" Willow muttered, but knew it was a dick thing to say.

"Your dad's right to be worried."

Willow tipped her head backward and blew a sigh to the heavens as her eyes burned. "He won't let me in to apologize," she said.

"I will," Wes said.

He'd come into the kitchen to join their coffee klatch. Willow glanced at the brown bottle in her hand. Beer klatch.

"Just not today, Willow. Elena says she should sleep the rest of the night. You can talk to her in the mornin'."

His voice had changed, Willow thought, shooting a quick glance at Drew to see if she'd noticed it, too. Drew furrowed her brow to acknowledge she had.

"I'm really sorry, Dad. I didn't know." Willow felt like shit for hurting her mother. In her defense, she thought, her mother had never seemed hurtable.

Her dad nodded. "I shouldn't have kept it from you," he said. "If I'd just told you privately, it could've stayed between us and maybe she wouldn't have—"

"No, it couldn't." She cut him off in a harsher tone than she'd intended. "Dad, you can't think it was *ever* okay to keep this secret from any of us. This isn't just about you and Mom. The whole family deserves to know the truth."

"Well, thanks to you, now they do."

"That's not fair, Uncle Wes." Little Drew stepped right up to Will's tall, lean father and tipped her chin up. "We younger Brands are more like siblings than cousins. We all deserved to know that one of us was missing."

"Dead." Wes Brand dropped the word like a cinder block. *Thud.*

"Not without a body, he's not," Drew snapped back.

Wes pointed a forefinger right at her. "No. You hear me, niece? You do *not* mess around in this, Drew Brand. You are not a detective. You're a kid."

"I have a license that says otherwise, Uncle Wes, and twenty-three is not a kid. I took that accelerated course last summer and passed my exam with flying colors. Tied for first in the class."

"That's all well and good, but if you go digging into this, you'll tear your Aunt Taylor's heart right out of her chest," Wes said. His black hair bore strands of white and was pulled back in its customary band. "You need to leave this alone, both of you."

Drew stepped back, holding up her hands as if in surrender. But there was a spark in her eyes that hadn't died. Willow saw it clearly, but she didn't think her father did.

"The things is, Dad," she said, "I don't think you get to tell me what to do about this. I don't think I'm the one in the wrong here. I need more information. I want to know everything about my brother. Mom doesn't have to know about it if you think she can't handle it. I think she can, but if you don't, I can keep secrets, too. Apparently, it runs strong in our line."

Her father lowered his head, shaking it, clearly angry and trying to bank it. He said, "I'm going upstairs. Come back in the morning. *Late* morning. You can talk to her then."

"Fine." Willow chugged the beer and slapped the bottle onto the counter, then started for the back door, because her father was between her and the front.

"Fine," he said. And then as she opened the door, he added, "I love you," the words clipped.

"Me, too." Then she was out. Drew followed, but Elena stayed behind, speaking softly to Wes about the meds she was leaving in case Taylor needed them. The door closed behind them.

Drew slung an arm around Willow's shoulders, which was awkward as she was several inches shorter than Willow.

"We're not fixin' to leave this alone, are we, Will?" she asked.

"Not in this lifetime," Willow replied.

Wolf

Wolf stood beside an open grave. They'd lined the inside of the hole with green felt, so the dirt wouldn't show. His young, beautiful, vibrant, secretive mother was in the box suspended above the hole. He felt as hollow as the grave.

Cilla had made all the funeral arrangements herself, and she'd kept it modest but dignified, choosing a black casket with white lining and dark bronze hardware. She'd bought a plot in the middle of a small cemetery and had made arrangements for her life insurance policy to pay for all of it, with the remainder going to Wolf.

Unbelievable.

She'd even planted a tree on the spot ahead of time.

She'd always been fiercely independent, his mother. She'd dated. A lot. But as soon as any of them started to get serious, they were history. Serious, she'd told him once, usually meant possessive and controlling. So the minute one of them told her what to do, criticized a decision or how she spent her time, or treated her son badly, they were gone.

She'd loved him.

He was kind of amazed by his mom when he thought about it.

It was a beautiful day in the fifties and warm, more typical of the area than the snow of the other night, though they got a little snow every winter. His mom had loved the snow. She always treated it like a special occasion when it snowed. It was nice that it had been snowing the night she'd died.

The other waitresses she'd worked with at the diner were there. Two brought their spouses, and three were alone. A few of the regular customers had come, and two of Cilla's nurses showed up, too.

Camellia and her mother were there. He hadn't seen either of them since that night. It bothered him a little that Camellia was a P.I. who knew more about him than he knew about himself. He didn't like outsiders in his business.

She was wearing her hair up again. Always up, in a twisted, untidy nest of golden shades. It seemed like a lot of hair, and he'd wondered at least six times since he'd met her how long it was and whether she ever took it down.

He stood near the grave. The headstone was a short, thick slab with a hand-hewn effect. It stood low to the ground. On its downward-angled front, there was a brass plaque with her name, Cilla Travail, and her date of birth and death.

Wolf squinted and bent nearer. The date of birth—it was the date she'd run away from her abusive stepfather. August 10th, and the year she'd been fourteen years old.

"She didn't even want her family to find her in death, did she?" asked a soft voice.

Camellia had moved closer to him.

"I guess not," he said. He felt a little guilty that he hadn't called her about the case of his missing birth family. It had been a week. She must wonder why it was taking him so long to decide.

He had to look at her then. In her eyes, he saw compassion and maybe a few unshed tears. "I'm sorry I haven't reached out—" he began.

"You've got nothing to be sorry for. You're dealing with a lot. I'd be curled up in a corner somewhere."

"I don't think you would."

"If it were *my* mom? Are you kidding me?" She glanced over at the woman as she said it.

Erica Rio's eyes beamed kindness and comfort when she caught his, even though she was chatting with his mom's co-workers.

Camellia said, "I'd lose it. I know I would. We're so close. I can't even think about the fact that she's not getting any younger."

"Looks to me like she's got a couple of decades left in her, at least," he said. "Look at those pink cheeks. And she's a retired nurse. She knows how to take care of herself."

Camellia tipped her head to one side. Her messy bun of multi-hued hair slid a little sideways. "Are *you* trying to comfort *me*, Wolf? You're the one grieving. I'm just...empathizing, I guess."

"It's appreciated."

She lowered her head, then said, "Are you doing a whole reception thing at your house after, or...?"

"I didn't feel like I could...have folks in her space. She would've hated it."

"I picked up on that from her," she said, meeting his eyes again. "She hated having to tell me about her history. She was a very private person, wasn't she?"

"Extremely, yeah."

"I guess it makes sense, now that we know what we do. Have you done any more reading? Of the diaries?"

"A little. Mainly I've been talking with the funeral director and doing all the...things. There are a lot of things. Bank accounts, life insurance payout, the death certificate...with her legal name and actual birthdate, which I had, thanks to you."

She frowned at him.

"I got a packet of documents from the lawyer," he said.

"Oh. Yeah, I didn't have anything to do with that."

"Oh." He shrugged. "There was quite a bit of the insurance money left after the funeral expenses," he said. "I was thinking of upgrading her headstone."

"She knew there would be extra," Camellia said. "She told me to tell you she wants you to use it to fix up your truck."

He expelled an almost-laugh. "She *would* say that."

"It was one of her last wishes. I think you have to do it."

A hand on his arm made him turn. Camellia's mother had come to join them, and she gave his upper arm a gentle squeeze. "I'm so sorry for your loss, Wolf," she said.

"I know you are, Erica. Thanks for coming."

She looked at him, then around at folks all leaving, then back at him again. "Come for dinner. It's leftovers, but comfort food. Lasagna!"

"You don't have to do that, ma'am. I'm fine."

"Don't *have* to. Want to. Besides you can talk about the uh— the case, you know."

"*Mom.*" Camellia's tone was gentle, but warning.

"The case of your missing family," Erica went on. "Where are they? *Who* are they? You must want to know."

He lifted his head. "I don't know that I do. I mean, how did I get in that river? I find it pretty telling that they never even looked for me."

Camellia gasped. "What makes you think they never looked for you?"

He shrugged. "Well, they never *found* me, that's for sure."

"Maybe they tried their best." Her deep blue eyes became a stormy sea. "Maybe it broke their hearts when they failed."

"Sure would've broken mine," said her mother.

He hadn't thought of that, that his original family might have tried to find him or might have been heartbroken at his loss. He wondered why he'd gone straight to the opposite assumption.

"Well, I hope you'll say yes to dinner," Erica said. "Because that way Camellia will have a ride home."

He looked from the sly sixty-something to her daughter.

Camellia said, "I assumed we were going home together."

"Well, we were, but as long as Wolf is willing to give you a ride, I can make it to the ladies' club meeting. We're planning for our group cruise, you know."

"I thought that wasn't until seven."

"Don't argue with your mother, dear. So? Wolf? You'll drive her home?"

He blinked, taken by surprise at the rapidly shifting topic. "Yeah, sure I will."

"Good. The lasagna's in the fridge Camellia. Just enough for two. And there's pie for dessert!" Then she moved around the headstones and out to the parking lot so fast you'd have thought there were ghosts chasing her.

Camellia let her chin drop to her chest. "She's fixing us up."

"Is she?"

"Yes, despite that she knows it's the opposite of what I want."

"Oh." He didn't really know what to make of that statement and knew his "oh" had borne the distinct ring of disappointment.

"Don't take that personally," she said quickly. "I've sworn off men in general."

"Oh?" he said again, this time as a question.

"Look there's no pressure to drive me home. I can call a Lyft or—"

"My truck's right here," he said, and he shrugged. "Look, I got no interest in women right now anyway, so you're safe enough. And…I heard there was pie."

She lifted her eyes up to his. "My mother says pie makes everything better."

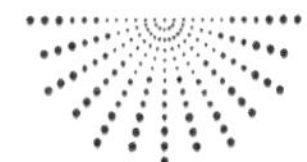

CHAPTER FOUR

CAMILLIA

"That was good," Wolf said later.

They were sitting at the small kitchen table in her mom's house, and their plates were empty. "I'm glad you enjoyed it. Mom makes a mean lasagna."

"I've been living on junk the past few days," Wolf admitted. "Mom did all the cooking. That meal had more vegetables than I've seen in a while."

"Was Cilla a good cook?" Camellia asked.

"No!" He said it with emphasis that made her laugh. Then he went on. "She got it wrong as often as she got it right, but I enjoyed our meals. Grandma Sage, now she could cook. I s'pose I'll have to learn to fend for myself now."

"I used to cook," she said. "I've been letting my skills slide lately, though. Living with Mom, I'm getting spoiled." She patted her belly. "And fat."

"I would too, with food like that," he said, smiling. Then he looked suddenly wide-eyed. "Not that I think you're fat."

"I don't care if you do," she reminded him. Only, she did, which was a problem. "So speaking if your Grandma Sage…?" she asked, raising her brows.

"I've been wondering about her, too, but I don't know. I s'pose it's in the journals," he said. "I have a photo." He took out his phone and scrolled and handed it to her.

The photo was of a little Native American boy, standing between his redheaded Irish mother and an old Black woman with white hair cut close to her head, in front of what looked like a petting zoo.

"That's Grandma Sage?"

"The one and only. The three of us could've been the start of a joke if we'd ever walked into a bar, I guess."

She handed him the phone.

They were quiet a moment, then she said, "Let's have coffee and dessert in Mom's parlor." She got up as she said it, went to the coffee maker, and turned it on. Her mother always left it ready to go.

Wolf got up too and started to clear the dishes while she sliced pie. She put it onto plates and stuck them in the microwave for 45 seconds. Then she got the vanilla bean ice cream from the freezer and a scooper from the drawer.

"You don't mean it." Wolf's deep voice sent a shiver right up her spine. The good kind. Well, the bad kind, considering her singlehood. She looked over her shoulder at him. He stood at the sink, rinsing plates. Beside him, the dishwasher was open and partly loaded.

"Oh, I mean it sincerely," she said, and the microwave beeped like an exclamation point. She took out the plates, dolloped a scoop of vanilla ice cream on top of each perfectly heated slice of apple pie, set a fork across each plate, and handed him one.

"That's…heaven."

"Close as we'll get on this side," she said. "Here's to Cilla." And she tapped the rim of her plate against his.

"To you, Ma." He smiled when he said it.

It startled Camellia and she realized she hadn't seen his smile before. She set down her plate and turned to put the ice cream away, and maybe hide her reaction to that smile.

After a beat, she took her plate, led him to the room her mother had always called the parlor, and tried to see it through his eyes.

There were filled bookshelves on three walls and five chairs that didn't match, each a different style and pattern. Equally diverse end tables stood beside each of the chairs. The furniture was all arranged to face a set of large French doors that led out onto the currently barren stone patio.

"There are usually lawn chairs out there," she explained, pointing. "But we put them in the shed when it's cold and wet like this. And the flowers are all gone till spring."

"It's a nice room." He nodded at the fireplace. "You want a fire?"

"Sure," she said, and then picked up a remote control from one of the end tables and aimed it at the fireplace. It lit up with fake flames that were nowhere near convincing. "It blows heat if you need it. There's a crackling sound effect, but it sounds tinny."

"Cheap speaker," he said, moving closer to the thing, bending low. "I could wire in a better one for you."

"No," she said. "Tell me you're not one of those."

"One of what?" He'd chosen a chair, the deep blue velour wingback with the peacock design. He put his plate on the oval cherry wood table-slash-magazine stand beside it, then took his first bite, closed his eyes and said, "Sorry. Couldn't wait."

She lowered herself into a Louis XV chair with ivory upholstery and pink roses on the other side of a '70s end table, and set her plate there. "I'm waiting for the coffee."

"Ice cream'll melt," he said.

"Only a little."

He took another bite, closed his eyes again. He was really into that pie. Watching him was too much, though. She bounced out of her chair and hurried back to the kitchen. Grabbing two cups, she filled them from the coffee maker's flow, swapping a cup for the carafe, and then for the other cup, then back to the carafe again without spilling a drop. It was better than waiting and watching him make love to that pie.

When she set their cups on their respective end tables, he said, "What did you mean by 'one of those'?"

"One of those guys who can fix things. A maker. A… MacGyver."

"You know MacGyver?" he asked, his eyebrows high.

"My mother still has the entire series on DVD. Bookcase on the right, top shelf."

He looked that way, then whistled and said, "Boxed set," as if impressed.

"Mom doesn't kid around about MacGyver. How do *you* know him? He's before your time, too."

"Grandma Sage," he said. "VHS."

Camellia laughed all the way from her belly, and in a second realized he was laughing, too. When they stopped, he was still smiling. He said, "You might be good for me, Camellia Rio."

A forbidden memory floated free of its prison, rising in tandem with the chill up her spine. *You're good for me, Camellia. You're the only good thing in my life. I'd kill you before I'd let you go. You know that, right?*

The sound of Wolf's fork against his plate as he set it down sent the ghost skittering back into the shadows. She closed her eyes like closing the door, shutting it in.

"What was that?" Wolf asked.

"What?"

"Something in your eyes just then. Was it because I said you're good for me?"

She shrugged. "I don't really want to be…good for anyone. I had a fiancé. He…needed me a little too much."

"How so?" Wolf was frowning, curious, maybe concerned.

"At first, just…hyper-attentive," she said. Because why not let him know right up front where she stood? If they were going to work together, she needed to set her boundaries firmly. "Later, he became controlling, suspicious, jealous. When I broke it off, he stalked me for three years."

"That's awful. I'm sorry, Camellia. Is it ongoing? Are you okay?"

She shrugged. "He stopped six months ago. I don't know why. I don't dare try to check up on him, because if he catches on that I did, it might reactivate the whole thing. It just…flashed through my mind when you said I was good for you. I know you didn't mean it that way."

"I could've phrased it better," he said. "What I meant was I enjoy your company. How's that?"

"Better." She nodded at his pie. "Finish up before it gets soggy."

Then she started eating her own to stop herself from talking. She probably shouldn't be sharing so much personal stuff. He was a client. A potential client. But he was so damn attractive to her that it seemed a good idea to be clear about where she stood on male-female relationships and why.

When they finished the last sips of coffee, he rose and said, "I should go. You've been kind, you and your mother both. I'm grateful."

Camellia stood up, too, tried to think of something to say and failed.

Wolf took his jacket from the hook near the door and draped it over his forearm. Head low, he opened the door.

She blurted, "I enjoy your company, too."

He lifted his chin and turned to face her again. He seemed pleased, but the sadness remained in his eyes. So she went on. "On a personal level, I mean. I really do. I wouldn't want you to think otherwise. It's just that…I'm not gonna take that risk again, you know? So, if we go forward with the case, we'd both need to be clear on that. First sign of anything...*you know*...and I'm gonna have to call it quits. I'd refund the fee, though, of course."

He studied her face for a long moment, frowning. It felt as if he was trying to see more than she was saying. "Look, Camellia, I don't even know my real name. It's like when Ma died, she took my whole identity with her. I'm not looking for...*you know*."

They locked eyes. A thunderbolt struck her speechless.

He put on his coat. "But I've decided that I *would* like you to go ahead and help me find my roots."

"*What?*" She thought they were addressing the slow simmer she felt between them, but maybe she was the only one feeling it. His sudden change of topic gave her mental whiplash.

"You do?"

He nodded.

"Are you sure?"

"No. Nervous as hell about it, to be honest." He lowered his head, a humble gesture. "I don't think I'll ever be sure, though," he said, looking her in the eyes once more. "So let's do this."

Her breath left her chest in a rush and she couldn't get it back for a second.

"Where do we begin, Detective?"

She tried not to smile too much. This was serious, and his mother had just been buried.

"We'll begin at the beginning. We have to look for a missing newborn around the time of that flash flood, upstream from where you wound up. That location, I hope, is in your mother's diaries. It shouldn't be hard. We'll start with the internet." She saw the hesitation in his eyes, then added, "But not tonight. I need to hit the treadmill and then the shower."

"No way am I working off *my* dessert," he said and rubbed his belly like an older, fatter man might do. "I want to keep it for a while. So when do we start, then?"

Tomorrow sprang to her lips, but she didn't let it escape. "I'll call you," she said.

"Okay," he replied. Then he looked at her for a long moment, blinked slowly, and gripped the doorknob again. "Thanks, Camellia. It was nice to not go home to the empty house tonight."

"For me, too, what with Mom's suddenly early ladies' club meeting."

"Yeah." He laughed softly, opened the door, and went outside. "Thank your mom for me, too."

"Goodnight, Wolf," she said, and closed the door.

WOLF

Wolf went home, but it didn't feel like home. It felt like a lie. The place was empty and lifeless without his mom.

Under the spray of a hot shower, he replayed the day. He'd done a bone-headed thing tonight, telling Camellia to go ahead with the search for his missing family. He hadn't intended to. He'd been debating whether he ever would. But something had happened.

She'd made him laugh on the worst day of his life, and he'd felt something between them. As if the sounds of their laughter had intertwined and woven themselves together.

And then she laid down the law about having no interest in men, and he'd realized not letting her help him meant not seeing her again at all, maybe. And that had instigated panic.

Telling her to go ahead and find his birth family had been a knee-jerk reaction. And now he was committed. Or maybe he *should be* committed.

Maybe it would be all right, though. Maybe she wouldn't find anything. He hoped to God she didn't find anything. But maybe...

it would take a little time for her to give up, and in the meantime...

What?

He didn't know. He wondered if pretending he wanted to find his family just to get to see her again would put him in the same category as her stalker-ex in her eyes. It had been stupid.

He hadn't been lying when he'd told her he was in no shape to be thinking about women right now, but he was thinking about her.

He wondered about that. Her history, the ex. It must've been bad to have her swearing off men forever. He wondered what the guy had done to her and felt a darkness cross his soul. Then he realized that thinking about Camellia had distracted him from thinking about the rug being ripped from underneath his own life. He couldn't remember feeling such an instant interest in a woman before.

Maybe it was good that she'd drawn a boundary line between them. It was protecting him from himself.

It wasn't lost on him that she was the first woman in his life since the most important one had left it. Maybe that was all this was.

He toweled down and went to bed, but he knew he'd never sleep. So he returned to the unfinished diary on his nightstand.

CILLA

August 11

I've been digging through some of the cargo to pass the time. I found a box of aluminum baseball bats stacked top to bottom, and there were multiple boxes just like it. Another one has golf clubs packed in individual Styrofoam forms like they're precious. But the best thing I found was camping gear. No food, no clothes. I wish there'd been time to grab some clothes from my bedroom. I keep thinking about all my stuff, all my jeans, my jacket, my shoes.

Anyway, I found a case full of tents in sacks that seem way too small to hold one. I took one. It says "two-person dome tent" on the front. Found a sleeping bag, too, still in shrink wrap. It's marked "teen" and covered in Mutant Ninja Turtles. There are crates of them.

I unwrapped and unrolled the sleeping bag, then rolled it back up with the tent and my pillow and blanket in the middle. Then I used the elastic bands on the sleeping bag to attach it to my backpack, and pulled them both over my shoulders.

I'm making the next stop the end of my ride. I don't care where we end up. I think it's far enough and I'm ready to get out of this—

Wait, we're stopping. Okay, more later.

HOLY GOD, that was scary!

I have to write it down while it's fresh, even before I go to sleep.

I heard him coming around the truck, so I took hold of my bike's handlebars and lifted it up off its side a little bit, listening, waiting.

Suddenly the tarp was yanked right off the truck, and I stood there in full-on daylight! The driver was a big guy with a dark beard, plaid shirt, and wide eyes. He said, "What the hell?" and I just straddled the bike and pushed hard on the pedal and shot right off the tailgate. I hit the ground without tipping over. I didn't even think about it then, I was so scared, but now it seems kind of amazing. Right then all I could do was keep on pedaling.

After a while, I realized nobody was coming after me, and I eased up a little. I figure I rode that bike for two hours under the hot, Texas sun.

Yep, I made it to Texas. I finally saw enough road signs to figure out that much. I was far away from that piece of shit my mother married—

out of his reach. But man, I was tired. And hungry again. At least I had a place to sleep because I was carrying it on my back.

After a while, I saw a sign that said Big Bend National Park, and I headed that way. The place looked peaceful.

It reminded me of back when I was little and my family used to go camping at a place called Port Ontario. It was "up north" from where we lived. I remember those trips well. It was before Dad started doing things to me. We used to fish for bullhead. He baited my hooks and taught me to cast. I was so proud when I caught a fish.

I adored him. I didn't even know he was my stepdad back then. He was just Dad.

But I don't like thinking about those things. I think I'll lock the door on those memories and throw away the key. I don't need them anymore, not down here. This is a brand new life for me, a brand new start.

The entrance to the park was a narrow, paved road with a set of open gates. There was a gatehouse with a person inside, so I stopped out of sight to watch.

One by one, cars and trucks drove up to the gatehouse, paid some money, got a ticket, and then drove into the park. Some of them were towing campers behind them.

I figured they wouldn't let a kid my age in there all alone, at least not without calling a cop to come check up on me. So I waited until nightfall, when the lady left the gatehouse and closed the gates. Cars only went in this way, never came back out, so I guessed there must be a different spot where cars left the place again.

I watched closely. I hadn't come this far to get caught.

The gate lady wore dark green shorts, a button-down shirt, had brown curls, and a fun ranger hat hanging on her back from its strap around her neck. She was smiling for no reason as she walked into the park along its neat, narrow lane.

I walked my bike over the pavement and rolled right on inside. There was room around the outside of the gate. I didn't need to open it, just needed a little privacy. I got on my bike and rode in the same direction the park ranger had gone.

The lane forked in two places and I had no idea where I was going. There were patches of scrubby brush here and there, but the landscape was mostly rock. I'd expected a forest in a national park. Home felt further away than ever.

A car came my way and there was no time to hide. My heart about pounded through my chest. I saw the driver—that gate lady with her curly brown hair. She looked right at me, then she smiled, and waved, and kept on driving.

I almost floated off my bike seat in relief! I guess there's nothing unusual about a girl with a pack on her back, riding a bike in a national park. I was still invisible.

So I found a spot behind some boulders that can't be seen too easily from the road, away from other campers, and I pitched my little tent. It looked way more complicated than it turned out to be. I took off my shoes before I came inside and unrolled my sleeping bag, laid out my pillow, put my blanket over top. I even rolled my bike inside for safe-keeping.

And now I'm curled up. I'm still hungry but even more sleepy, and I'm warm and safe. I'm even pretty comfortable. So I'm going to sleep now. My first night in Texas! And I don't think I need to worry about anybody in this park coming into my tent to paw me in my sleep.

WILLOW, SKY DANCER RANCH

Willow arrived in her mom's living room to find her sitting on the sofa, waiting. There was an antique strongbox from the old west beside her. It had "Pinkerton" stamped on one side. She thought Drew would've given a limb to have it.

Drew was planning to start her own PI business with her brother Orrin. Until they pulled the trigger on that, they both worked for their mother's investigations agency and freelanced here and there.

Drew was a born snoop. She'd been named after Nancy Drew.

There was a tea service on the coffee table. Her mom's native-made clay set, and a plateful of small cookies she had not made herself. Willow spotted Fig Newtons, Chips Ahoy, and Oreos.

Her mother looked up when she heard her come in. Her eyes were so puffy and red that Willow gasped in surprise before she could prevent it. Then she moved faster, suddenly swamped in regret. She dropped to her knees in front of her mom. "I'm so sorry, Mom. I'm so sorry. I was angry and I felt betrayed. But I didn't mean to hurt you. I'd never want to hurt you."

Her mother petted her head as if it were a cat in her lap. "You had a right to feel angry and betrayed. I've kept this from you, and that was wrong. But no more." She gripped Willow's shoulders and straightened her. "I want you to know everything, my Willow. And it's all here."

As she spoke, she caressed the lid of the strongbox, and then she raised it.

Willow sank onto the sofa beside her as her mother reached into the box, then paused. Her hands were shaking.

Willow leaned forward to cover them with her own. "Are you sure you can handle this?"

Taylor nodded rapidly. "It's time." Then she pulled out a baby book and laid it on the table between them. Its cover was padded fabric with rearing mustangs, and when she opened the book, Willow gulped. There was her mother, so much younger, in a hospital bed, holding a tiny newborn baby. He had a thick head of black hair, a comically turned-up nose, and intense brown eyes. He looked like a wise, nut-brown elf who knew all the secrets of the universe.

"What's that on his wrist?"

"A bracelet. Made by a shaman as a gift."

"Shaman? What shaman?" Willow asked.

Taylor smiled, her gaze turning inward. "Turtle. An old friend of your father's. We thought he'd passed, but...it arrived at the hospital within minutes of his birth with a blank card that had a turtle on it." She focused on the photo again. "Your dad put it on him the day he was born. A bond to his family, clan, and tribe. See the wolf stone in the center?"

"I see it."

"When your father put it on him, he..." Her mother made a soft sound and Willow turned to her. "Maybe I can't do this after all," she whispered. "I'm sorry, Willow. I'm sorry. Can you...?" She closed the book and dropped it back into the strongbox atop baby blankets and clothes. "Just take it, can you? I can't..."

She got up, and Willow did, too.

Her mother hugged her. "Sorry, honey. I love you." Then she turned and went to the staircase and up it without looking back.

Willow closed her eyes and swore under her breath. Sighing, she texted Drew.

> Project Wolf. Meet at my OLD place ASAP

Drew responded with a thumbs-up emoji.

Willow left her mom's house, carrying the strongbox in front of her. It was heavy, but not from its contents. The box itself was heavy.

By the time she'd trudged down the long stretch of driveway between her parents' house and the guest cottage where she'd lived before moving in with Jeremiah, Drew was already pulling in.

Her rusty gray 1988 VW Jetta with its squared off headlights and boxy grill rumbled closer. It was the most fuel-efficient model she could afford on her own income. Drew parked and jumped out, then ran ahead to open the cottage door. "What is it?"

"Everything, I think." Willow carried the box inside with

Drew on her heels. She set it on the coffee table and took off the lid. "Mom started to show me, then she kind of lost it." Her throat convulsed so hard it hurt. "I've never seen her like this."

"You messed up. You know that, right?" Drew moved through the place like she owned it, heading into the kitchen, opening the fridge. Willow didn't live there, but she still kept supplies on hand for cousin meetings and the like.

Drew came back with two Cokes, passing one to Willow before dropping onto the sofa.

Willow took the baby book out of the box, set it on the coffee table, then looked to see what else was inside. Baby blankets, baby clothes, booties, a little plastic hospital bracelet with "Jonathon Wolf Brand" on it.

Drew was turning pages in the baby book. "His birth certificate. Oh, look, his little footprints!"

Willow set the hospital bracelet down and scooted closer to Drew as she turned pages. So many shots of that baby boy. That other bracelet, the one gifted to him by a shaman, was on his chubby wrist in every single photo. There were shots of Willow's dad holding him, Willow's mom holding him, and the three of them posing in the most beautiful baby-makes-three shots ever taken. Dozens of photographs of Johnny Wolf with each of his uncles and most of his aunts, each photo with his age underneath in days.

They didn't go past fifteen.

The last photo was of him in a car seat in the back of an SUV Willow had never seen, with "Sky Dancer Ranch" painted on the side. Underneath, it said, *Fifteen days old and ready for his first checkup.*

God, that had to be his final day. "Drew!"

Drew jumped, startled. "What?"

"I think this is the day it happened. On his way for his first checkup."

"Oh God," Drew whispered, leaning nearer the photo.

Taylor was smiling in the picture, crouched beside the car near the car seat in that very driveway Willow just walked, while someone else took the shot.

"That's heartbreaking," Drew said. "Wait, is he wearing a bracelet?"

One pudgy baby hand had extricated itself from the woven receiving blanket in which the baby was swaddled, as if reaching for the camera. Wrapped around his wrist was that leather bracelet, lined in beads, white with blue around the edges, and the name "WOLF" spelled out in turquoise and carnelian. The letter O was a moonstone with an intricately carved wolf's head in its face.

Drew pulled out her phone and took a photo of the printed photograph. "A scan would be better, but later. This is good for now."

"The bracelet's native-made," Willow said. "A gift from a shaman, Mom said."

"The blanket's Native too, and distinctive," Drew added.

"We found the blanket," said a deep voice. Willow's dad had come in and stood in the open door of the guest cottage. "It was tangled on some branches in a stretch of rough current, way downriver."

"But no baby," Willow whispered.

Wes shook his head, slow and sad. "Rangers said wildlife prob'ly…" He closed his eyes, shuddered.

Drew whispered, "Where, Uncle Wes? Where, *exactly*, was the blanket found?"

The way his eyes looked when he opened them compelled Willow to add, "We want to do a ceremony for him. Just us cousins."

Wes's eyes focused on hers, and she knew he was looking for the lie. She held his gaze, defiant. He couldn't stop her from trying to find out what had happened to her brother. She wouldn't let him stop her. Her mom didn't have to know.

They were locked that way, in ocular combat, until Wes sighed and said, "It's right at the border of Big Bend. Rapids after that. Even if he made it that far, there's no way he could've..." Again, he let his words trail off. "A ceremony'll be good for you, I guess. Maybe you need it. Just...don't mention it to your mother."

"Is she okay?"

Wes nodded. "She's stronger now than she was back then. Hell, that experience is probably what *made* her stronger once she...came back to herself." He met Willow's eyes and his were bleak. "For a while I wasn't sure she would. I thought I'd lost the both of 'em." He reached out and pushed Willow's long, dark hair behind one ear. "You're so much like her. You healed us when you came along. As much as we could be healed. You're our miracle. Never doubt it."

"Oh, Dad." She rose and hugged him and he hugged her back.

"If you have questions, you can ask me. I'm not mad at you. You have a right to know about your brother."

She pressed her lips and nodded against his shoulder. "Thanks, Dad."

"The thing is, uh, if you do go diggin', there won't be much to find."

"What do you mean?" Drew was the one who asked.

Willow was too busy trying to put it together in her mind.

"Your mom was falling apart. The flood took her baby right out of her arms and that was just too good a story. If it'd hit the papers or the townsfolk had known—she couldn't have handled that. So we kept it quiet."

"That's what Uncle Garrett said," she murmured.

"Garrett being Sheriff helped. He could have every resource out there looking for him without it being front-page news. We told folks he'd passed, and that was all. Most assumed SIDS, and we let 'em."

"But, Dad, couldn't the press have helped?" Willow asked, the breaks in her words echoing those in her heart. "What if someone found him or something?"

He lowered his head. "You don't know how much we prayed for that. And Garret left no stone unturned. But once we found the blanket, we knew." When he raised his head again, his eyes were wet. "You'll see."

CAMELLIA

Camellia left the public library, jogging down the steps to the sidewalk, taking out her favorite hair pin on the way. It was six inches long and made of jade. She'd been nine years old and on a family vacation, seeing the sights in San Francisco with her mom and dad. She'd spotted a whale on that trip and seals basking in the ocean. They'd stopped at a souvenir shop in Chinatown.

Camellia's hair had been long her entire life, way beyond her shoulders. She loved her hair and rarely cut it. But it had been hot that day, and she remembered wishing she'd brought a scrunchy to put her hair up.

The shop was cool, and everything in it was fascinating, exotic, and bright. There were dragons in red and black and green, and statues of milky white glass, and fans and vases and fountains. She'd been admiring the hairpins in the glass case, particularly the jade, with the intricate carvings all along its length and Chinese letters spelling out words.

"You like the hairpins?" asked an elderly woman, probably the owner.

"Yeah, but they'd never work for me," she'd said. "Too much hair." She'd shaken her locks a little as she'd said it.

"You just have to know how. Come here. Sit right here. I'll

show you." As she said it, the old woman opened the case and took out the jade hairpin Camellia had been admiring.

She'd sent an eager smile her mom's way, and got the go-ahead nod. So she scooted up onto the small stool the lady had indicated. There was a mirror on a stand on the counter, and the lady turned it around so Camellia could watch her work.

She gathered her hair up, twisted it around, but not tightly, and wove the hairpin in and out and through, resulting in a delightfully messy bun. "There, you see? Easy." The whole thing had taken about three seconds.

Camellia had loved the look and adopted it on the spot.

"What are the words?" she'd asked.

"Love fearlessly."

"Good words," her dad had said, pulling out his wallet. "It looks too pretty on her to leave behind."

As she tapped over the sidewalk in front of the library, heading back to her car, Camellia caught her hair in both hands, smoothed it, re-twisted it, and stuck the hairpin back through. It had become a habit to undo and redo the messy bun. No two were ever alike. She sometimes did it to channel frustration, and she was definitely frustrated.

She'd found absolutely nothing about a missing baby. The flood, yes, and the timing of it fit, but no mention of a missing baby

"How can there not be anything?"

She wanted to see Wolf again. She wanted it more than was smart and more than was healthy. It had been three days and her eagerness to see him worried her, because she was determined they could only be friends. She would not put herself in harm's way ever again.

They could be friends only. And that could work. She liked him; he was easy to be around. But she needed a *reason* to see him, and she hadn't found a thing. Nothing. No mention in any newspaper of a missing baby anywhere upstream of the park around the time of the flash flood. She'd turned up nothing on the net either. It was weird, was what it was.

Could Cilla have lied?

It seemed unlikely she'd go to all the trouble to falsify those journals twenty-eight years ahead of time. Okay, so what if she didn't lie, what if she just got her facts wrong?

Maybe poor Wolf hadn't washed down the river at all. Maybe somebody had left him there, close enough to a campsite to ensure he'd be found. It was a weird way to abandon a baby, but it seemed more likely than a newborn surviving a trip down the Rio Grande without a boat.

She'd said he was a newborn, but Camellia wondered if a fourteen-year-old girl would be very good at guessing a baby's age.

She took out her key fob and unlocked her car. Her phone rang as soon as she did, and she took it from her shoulder bag while sliding behind the wheel, glanced at the number, which she did not recognize, and answered it anyway. Could be a new client. "You've got Camellia Rio," she said.

"Who is he?" said the voice she'd hoped to never hear again.

Frost formed over her veins. She found the end call button with her thumb and threw the phone away from her, onto the passenger seat, wanting to wash her hands.

It immediately rang again. And again. She waited until it stopped and then, her hands shaking, she reached across the car to pick the phone up. She turned it to face her and tapped on the dots beside recent calls. The dropdown menu included "BLOCK CALLER."

It rang again before she could touch it, and it startled her so badly she hit answer instead of end. And in the instant she realized it, her fear turned to anger, rose up in her chest, and exited in a rush through her lips. "Leave me alone, you fucking psychopath!"

"Whoa, whoa, whoa, hey..."

It was not the voice she'd expected. It was Wolf's voice. She closed her eyes, whispered his name with a question mark after. "Wolf?"

"Where are you?"

"Public library. Parked in front."

"Okay, I know the area. Go around the block. There's a bar on the other side, Joe's Place. I'll be there in five."

She looked around and wondered if Earl was out there watching her the way he used to. Or at her house, watching it and her mom. Her mom!

"I'll wait here instead. Parking's crap over there. Pick me up?" The truth was she didn't trust herself to drive. Her hands were shaking. Her heart was racing.

There was the slightest hesitation before he replied, "Sure. Sure I will, Camellia. I'll be there soon."

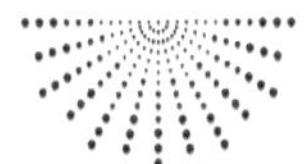

WOLF

olf had pulled the phone away from his ear when Camellia had answered it the way she had. Who the hell had she thought he was? She'd sounded furious, and then, after she realized it was him, shaky. She was scared.

He drove to the library. He'd already been in town, so it wasn't far. He didn't even park, just pulled up beside her car.

She got out the driver's door and re-locked it. Then she hopped into his passenger side quickly and gave a good look around them before she focused on him.

Her eyes didn't look right—wide with pinpoint pupils. He put the truck into gear, but he didn't drive around the block to Joe's. She sent him a question with her eyes. Dang, those eyes hit him hard every time they latched on. He thought there ought to be a ricochet sound effect.

"I thought of a better spot. The Dark Pony. Out of town, quieter."

"Okay."

"Because you seem nervous here."

"Do I?"

"Your head's on a swivel like you're a war vet with PTSD."

She finally looked at him and some of the fear left her eyes. She closed them, then took a deep breath and released it. "Well, the PTSD part's right. Just hasn't acted up in a while."

"And why's it acting up now, Camellia?"

She pressed a hand to her chest, tucked her chin, and took slow, measured breaths, blowing each one out through pursed lips. After several of them, she said, "My ex called."

"The stalker?" He went dark. That was the only way to describe the feeling that descended on him.

"I don't know how he got the number. It's unlisted. I answered, not knowing it was him."

"What did he say?"

"He said, 'who is he?'"

"Who is he," Wolf repeated. To his own ears, his voice had gone an octave lower.

"I think he meant you. I haven't been around any other *he* of late. I hung up, but he called right back. I was about to block his number when you called." She lowered her head. "Sorry I yelled at you."

"I just wish *he* could've heard it," he said. "I wouldn't mess with a woman who sounded like that, nossir. So you finished blocking the number, right?"

"Yeah, and I'll have to change mine. I know the drill. This is a violation of the restraining order, too, so I'll report it."

Wolf's emotions were more tumultuous than their short acquaintance called for. He couldn't sort that out and didn't try, because he needed to focus on Camellia. He could deal with his own feelings on his own time. She'd seemed really scared. But also appeared to be getting past her panic. "Does he know where you live?"

"I didn't live with Mom when we broke up, but he knows

where *she* lives." Catching her lower lip between her teeth, she frowned, then said, "I was thinking the same thing, then remembered she's not home. She and her bestie are shopping for their group cruise, then flying to Galveston to spend the night in a fancy hotel. They board the ship tomorrow morning."

"Are you saying you have the place to yourself and your mom is out of town?" He asked the question with a playful wiggle of his eyebrows he instantly regretted. No flirting. She'd drop him like a hot potato. "Just kidding." It sounded lame, tacked on the end like that. "Here we are." He steered the old truck into a packed-dirt parking lot with only a handful of vehicles in it. The building was a slab-sided rectangle, and music spilled from its swinging doors. In a wide front window, a neon sign said "Dark Pony," and the Y's tail flickered like a signal light with a broken fuse.

"It's quiet enough here," he said. "You can see everybody in the place, and sit with your back to the wall. Okay?"

"Perfect. Thanks for being so thoughtful."

"Sure." He opened his door and got out, then went around to open hers, but she was already hopping to the ground. They headed inside. It was dark and cool, and a thin band of tobacco smoke hung low. The hardwood bar was short, backed by a shelved mirror where the bottles lived. A Mexican woman stood behind it, filling a stein with beer from a tap. There were six stools in front and little round tables all around. The jukebox to the left of the entrance was silent. Another woman moved around the floor, delivering orders to the folks at the handful of occupied tables.

Wolf found a table in a shadowy corner in the back, with a full view of the room. She sat down, and then he did. The waitress showed up immediately. "What can I get for you?" she asked in a heavy Spanish accent.

"Brazos, if you have it on tap," Wolf said, naming his favorite beer. Then he asked Camellia, "Two?"

"*Quiero un whisky. Doble. Con hielo.*"

The server smiled, but she made no comment as she left to get their drinks.

"So you speak Spanish," he said.

"Badly. No doubt to our server's amusement, but I like to practice with real people when I can."

Wolf leaned back in his seat and said, "Have you seen any sign of him?"

Camellia had been scanning the patrons since they'd sat down. He'd taken a quick survey himself. The guys on the barstools along the front of it were regulars, he'd bet. They chatted and called the bartender by name. The rest of the folks at tables and the pair at the pool table seemed harmless. He watched her big eyes sweep the place, then she gave a nod, and her body seemed to lose a little of its stiffness.

Their server came back with their drinks. When she set Camellia's down, she said, "*Estoy aquí hasta las diez si me necesitas.*" Then she slipped away with a narrow look at Wolf that he felt clear to his toes.

"What did she say?" he asked.

"She's on until ten if I need her," she replied. "I wonder why she—"

"She thinks it's me," he said, when she was out of earshot.

"She thinks what's you?"

"She can see you're scared and nervous, and I'm the nearest guy to you, so—"

"Oh, hell, I'm sorry, Wolf."

"It's all right. Hell, it's fine. If I had a sister and she walked into a bar with some guy looking scared as hell, I'd want her server to look out for her."

"It's not my intention to be so obvious. Or so scared." She tried to school her face, but in doing it frowned so hard it made him smile. Then she rolled her eyes, took a mighty slug from her glass of whiskey on the rocks, and coughed most of it back out again. "Hooo—that's strong!" She mopped up the table with a napkin, then took a more moderate sip.

"You want to talk about it?" he asked.

"No. I really don't."

"Okay. You want to eat some unhealthy bar food?"

"I do. Yes."

He signaled the waitress and she gave them the sign for just a sec. Then Camellia said, "I used to have to watch for Earl everywhere I went. He'd just show up, at the drugstore or the gym. I'd see him lurking at the bank, or grocery store. He'd stand outside my apartment, under a streetlight to make sure I'd see him. He'd call and call. Every time I changed my number, he'd get it again. All hours of the night, he'd call and tell me the sick shit he was going to do to me one of these nights, to teach me a lesson. For leaving him, I guess." She shivered and rubbed her arms. "I never knew whether he was just trying to terrify me or if he was going to really do it, really hurt me, you know?"

Wolf swore softly, sounding a little like his mom, he thought.

Camellia took another slug of the whiskey. Apparently, she'd got used to the burn, because it was bigger than the first one and she didn't spew it back out this time.

"You didn't tell me why you were calling," she said. "Just came to the rescue like a unicorn."

He frowned and wondered just how hard that whiskey was hitting her. "I was calling to ask why you weren't," he said. "Calling, that is."

"Oh?" She blushed a little. "But we both said neither of us were looking for—"

"About the case." Damn, he'd messed that up, and now she was embarrassed. He hadn't meant to do that. So he added, "And I don't know, I kind of missed your smiling face. You should've brought it along."

She smiled with her mouth only, and sarcastically at that.

He shook his head and said, "Not even close."

"Best I can do at the moment. Maybe after I finish this." And she took another swallow.

"So the reason you haven't called?" he prompted.

"Ah, right, the reason I haven't called is because I didn't have a good excuse—*reason*. Reason. Because the case hasn't really started yet. I haven't picked up a single lead. Nothing in the newspaper archives, nothing on the net." She shook her head in obvious frustration. "Maybe my nemesis was right and I suck as a detective."

"You have a nemesis?" Wolf raised his eyebrows and looked at her with new eyes. "I'm learning a lot about you today."

"We both took the same accelerated course for the PI licensing exam last year. We competed for mock cases. The tougher the case, the better the potential for a high grade, so we wanted the good ones, and we both knew which ones those were." She took another sip. The glass was almost empty.

He didn't say a thing. He didn't want to interrupt; she might stop talking if he did.

"Most of the people in that class couldn't tell a great case from a misdemeanor, but we could. It was first-come, first-served. You had to go to the instructor personally to choose a case file, and you never knew when the list would drop. He'd announce it at random on a class-wide message."

"Interesting instructor."

"It was the best part of the class," she said, smiling. "We pretended to hate each other, but deep down, I think we were both having a blast coming up with ways to delay each other when the cases opened up. I was, anyway."

Her smile was real again. He liked that. "What kinds of ways?"

The waitress came back with a bowl of mixed pretzels and peanuts. "You need another?" she asked Camellia in English.

"*No, gracias.*" She bit off a piece of a pretzel, then after swallowing, said, "Let's see, one time we were at the same party when the message went out. I saw it first, swiped her car keys from the key bowl, put them in the fridge." She laughed at the memory. "I texted her after I got the primo case and told her where they were. Another time, she got the message first, saw where I'd parked, and let all the air out of one of my tires, then she went in and grabbed the best case."

"This is getting really interesting," he said, laughing softly. "Who won this ongoing competition of yours?" he asked.

Camellia shook her head. "We agreed it was a tie and that our final grade would be the tiebreaker."

"And?"

"We got the exact same score. Perfect. One hundred percent, both of us."

"Have you seen her since?"

"Not since she flipped me off with a smile at the reception after we aced the licensing exam. I returned it with both hands and a *superior* smile."

"I see."

"So I won."

"Noted."

Her playful smile died and she said, "Maybe I should call her. Maybe she could help us figure this out. She's the only snoop I know who's as good as I am."

"I have absolute faith in you," he said. "Have you been in business long, then?"

"I haven't really started my business yet."

"Oh."

She glanced his way quickly. "Declared absolute faith a little soon, didn't you?"

"Not a bit."

"Why? You don't even know me."

The teasing lilt had left her voice. "Oh, I think I'm getting to know you pretty well," he said. "Highly competitive, holds a grudge long-term, likes her whiskey on ice, speaks Spanish, and not allergic to peanuts. You already have ideas about these road-blocks you've hit, I can see you do."

"I have a couple. But the main one sucks."

"What is it?"

"That Cilla's story was incorrect, either on purpose—which I feel is very unlikely since the whole tale is backed up in her diaries—or in some way she couldn't have known."

"Such as?"

"Maybe you got into the river some other way."

He lowered his head to hide the hurt that kept creeping in. "You mean, maybe someone left me there."

She bit her lip but nodded.

"I can't say I haven't been wondering the same thing." He took a long pull from his bottle. When he set it down, he said, "That was your main idea, you said. What are your others?"

"Just one really. We need to go back to Big Bend, where Cilla was staying when you were found. Work our way upstream with a stop in whatever towns got hit hardest by that flash flood."

"And do what?"

"Ask questions. Talk to the locals, the ones old enough to remember."

He pressed his lips and said, "I gotta say, I like that option better."

She smiled quickly. "Because the other one's too depressing?"

"Because the other one's the end of the story. And I'm not happy with that ending." He held her eyes for a long moment, but then someone dropped some change into the jukebox and started up a song.

He took her hand and pulled her out onto the floor, where nobody else was dancing. He didn't know why; he just did it. She came along laughing, and he led her through the simple, bouncing steps his mom and grandma had taught him as a little boy, part cha-cha, part jitterbug, Grandma Sage had said.

She picked up the steps quickly and was soon laughing with him on the floor.

Wolf felt better than he'd felt in ages, aside from the notion that he'd been thrown away like unwanted garbage as a baby.

The music stopped and a slow song came on; he was still holding her hands. They locked eyes. She shrugged and smiled, then slid her hands around his neck, so he moved his to her waist, and told himself the urge to pull her in closer was a very bad idea.

Then she pulled herself closer and rested her head on his shoulder. His breath whispered out of his lungs and for a second, he forgot to suck anymore back in. Then she picked her head up and said, "So you want to do it?" And before he could put his eyeballs back into their sockets, she added, "You want to head down to that national park on the border and try to find your origin story?"

His heartbeat hadn't slowed back to normal yet. "Yes. I do."

"Can you get away for a few days?" she asked. "Starting tomorrow?"

"Boss on my construction crew told me to take some down-time after I explained about my mom and all. Said he'd hold my spot for me for a couple more weeks, but after that, all bets are off."

"Well, heck, we oughtta be able to wrap this up in a couple of weeks. One way or another, we'll have reached the end of the line by then."

"And it'll get you outta town for a while," he said. "Give that ex time to cool off."

"I don't know why he left me alone for six months only to call again now," she said.

"But you could find out. I mean, you're a P.I."

The song wound down, and he walked her back to the table with his arm hanging lightly around her waist, resting on her hip. Casual, not intimate. But almost intimate. Maybe.

As she slid into her chair, she said, "Like I said, I was afraid to check up on him. If I slipped and he realized it, it might spur him to start up again."

"Well, he's started up again anyway, hasn't he?"

"Yeah, you're right."

"Here, use my phone. Then he won't know it's you." He handed his phone across to her. She tapped away while he waved at the waitress and asked for a refill on his beer.

Moments later, Camellia nodded. "Ahh, he was dating somebody else. Mary Jo Gallagher. He changed his status from "in a relationship" to "it's complicated" two weeks ago. Wait I'll check her social. Her sites are…oh my God."

The color had drained from Camellia's face and the fear he'd seen earlier returned to her eyes. She turned the phone his way.

"In memoriam," he read, beneath a photo of a pretty blonde.

Camellia had pulled out her own phone by then, and within few more seconds said, "Suicide. Hanged herself last weekend. Body was found in the woods about five miles from her home. She left a note stuck to the tree."

"Holy God," he said. "He drove her to suicide?"

"Maybe." She lifted her gaze to his. "Or maybe it's a damn good idea for me to get out of town for a while. Can you, um…be ready tomorrow?"

"I can. But—and don't take this wrong. I swear I'm not violating our agreement—are you gonna be okay alone tonight?"

"Of course I am."

Camellia

Camellia didn't sleep a wink. Every time the wind rattled a shutter or a pipe groaned, she thought it was Earl coming after her. She'd changed her phone number and notified the police last night, first thing, before staying awake all night long.

It was okay, though. She'd had a lot of preparing to do. Like dragging Dad's camping duffle down from the attic. Thing was four feet long and packed like a jigsaw puzzle. She packed a smaller bag for herself and did some online research, too.

In the morning, she couldn't wait to get out of there. She had the most horrible feeling that Earl was going to jump out at her just before she managed to get away, and it was terrifying. She didn't mean to leave rubber on the pavement in front of the house, but she did anyway.

She drove to the usually bustling village parking lot in town. It wasn't bustling yet, because it was too dang early. You could barely tell it was daytime, the sky was so overcast.

They'd decided to take Wolf's truck on the drive down to Big Bend, as it was more reliable than hers. Oh, her little Civic was solid, but all the routine maintenance stuff her dad used to take care of for her hadn't been done since he'd passed, and she knew it was past due for a lot of it.

She didn't want to leave her car at her mother's. If her car wasn't there, Earl would assume she wasn't either and stay away. Even though her mom would be safe on her cruise for the next ten days, she didn't want Earl sniffing around her place.

She found a parking spot out of the way and pulled in, then taped a pre-written note to her windshield. "Not abandoned. Please don't tow. Back in a week."

She was leaning over, smoothing the tape to her windshield when she heard the rumbling sound of Wolf's pickup. That old truck sounded way better than it looked, that was for sure. She turned to watch as he drove right up behind her car and rolled his window down with a hand crank. His long black hair was pulled back in a band today, and his smile was warm. He wore a black felt cowboy hat, pushed back on his head.

"Morning," he said.

"Morning." She grabbed the normal-sized backpack and the giant-sized duffel bag from her car and slung them into the back of his pickup, then went around to the passenger side and climbed in.

"You good?" he asked.

She noticed how closely he was looking at her. He wondered if she'd heard from Earl, she realized.

"I'm good. Got a new number immediately, as you know from our texts this morning."

"Got it. Saved it. Didn't use your real name in my phone either."

"No? What did you use?"

"Veronica Mars," he said.

She rolled her eyes and laughed softly as he drove away from the village, heading south. "I talked to Mom. They're already the cruise ship, which leaves port at nine."

"That's good. I was worried." He handed her a coffee from the console. "Place all locked up?"

"Like a vault." She took a sip, said, "Mmm," and took another. "I talked to Detective Simms last night. She was the one who helped me before, when Earl was everywhere I looked."

"And you told her? About the girlfriend's suicide?"

She nodded while drinking coffee, then lowered the cup and said, "She hadn't heard. No reason she would, I guess. But she's interested now. Said she'd keep me posted, and she's been pretty good about that in the past."

"Good. Also good that we're getting you the hell away from here."

"Hell, yes." She glanced behind them as she said it. "Latest registration in his name is a Chevy Blazer, 1990. Probably the same one he had last year. It's jacked with flat black paint."

"That should be easy to spot."

She twisted around in the seat, bringing up one knee, watching the traffic behind them.

Wolf reached over and touched her shoulder, and she looked at him instead. "You can take a breath now."

She looked at him, nodded, smiled a little.

"Have you been this nervous all night? Did you even sleep?"

"Not really."

"You should've called, Camellia. You could've crashed in Mom's room."

She glanced at him quickly, and he must've seen the slight alarm in her eyes, because he went on quickly. "We're friends, aren't we? I feel like we are."

She pressed her lips, nodded. "It's a new friendship, but yeah, I feel that way, too."

"Well, you're allowed to crash at a friend's place when you're scared and alone," he said. "I think it's in the rulebook."

He was really trying to put her at ease, and she was beginning to think he meant it. Maybe he didn't have any expectations from her beyond helping with the case. And becoming a friend.

"I had a long night, too," he said, maybe to change the subject.

"What kept *you* up?" Camellia asked.

He patted the dashboard. "Put in a new starter. Got her a brand-new battery, too. Tested the alternator just to be sure. We're in good shape for the drive."

She nodded, appreciating that, but her nerves didn't ease until they'd put a solid fifty miles between themselves, Hobbsville, and everything related to Earl.

At length and unprompted, she said, "He was a nice guy once. It was like something broke in his mind. All of the sudden, he was suspicious and controlling, always sure I was deceiving him one way or another. And he started hanging out with the worst group of guys, a bunch of gun-nut survivalist types. It was a relief, though, when he started going with them on their trips."

"Trips?"

"All over Texas. Wilderness training, he called it. They'd set up camp in one park or another, do some target shooting and survival shit. I swear it sounded like one of those Taliban training videos you see, except with white boys." She sighed, shaking her head. "God, I hope he didn't kill Mary Jo Gallagher."

"Tell you what," Wolf said. "I brought Ma's diaries." He reached across in front of her, popped open the glove compartment, and pulled out the red journal with a bookmark in it. "Why don't you read aloud while I drive?"

"Sure," she said. It touched her to be entrusted with his mother's words. So she opened to where he'd left off and began.

CHAPTER SIX

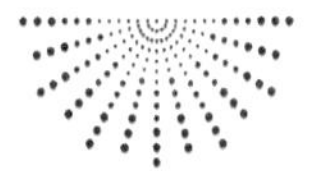

CILLA

September 15th

    Today was...I don't even know.

I haven't written in a while, so I have to get it all down. I want to remember this. Okay, so the park rangers have been starting to notice me, you know? They're not stupid. I've been here longer than anyone who was camping when I arrived.

I went out exploring for a new spot and I found the perfect place, hidden among the boulders on the shore of the river. The Rio Grande! I can hardly believe I'm here. It's a different world from New York. First off, everybody makes eye contact, smiles, waves. The first couple times it happened, I thought the person had a traumatic brain injury or some-thing. Childlike mind in an adult-sized body, that kind of thing. But no. It's everybody. It's freaking weird.

My new spot's outside the park boundaries, according to the map I picked up off the dash of a Jeep with the window left down. And yet it's still close enough that I can make regular trips back in to steal supplies.

It feels bad, writing that down. I steal, yes. I don't see that I have much choice about it. I don't feel like I had much choice about any of this. What else can I do, tell the authorities and wind up in a foster home? There was a girl in my English class who lived in one of those places, and she was a mess.

I try to be nice about my stealing. I never take more than one thing from a campsite, if I can help it, and I've scored some decent supplies—a little two-burner cook stove, a coffeepot, a cot, an air mattress, a couple of lanterns, shampoo, conditioner, soap, toothpaste, clothes, sandals and sneakers, and about a dozen of those mini-size tanks of propane.

Not to mention food.

People cook on grills and over campfires, and they always walk away long enough for me to grab a piece of whatever. I scored some good clothes from the campground laundry last week, after the mom of a girl about my size threw a load into the dryer and walked away.

I broke my own rule and took a pair of jeans, a pair shorts, and two T-shirts from her. I felt bad about that, but I was desperate for clothes that fit.

I found both pairs of shoes in the pool area. Kids leave them every-where. Towels, too, and sunglasses and water bottles.

I really would like some new books to read, so I'm on the lookout for careless readers.

My new spot is near a secluded spot by the river, where a skinny strand branches off behind a finger of ground, and a whole bunch of stuff washes up. Something about the current, I guess. I've been going there every day. I've found all sorts of things—a good denim jacket, soaked in mud and muck. A couple of cooking pots. A pair of boots with their laces tied together that were only a little bit too big.

So this morning, like the past few, I walked down to that spot. I was thinking how good the air smelled there, like the river washes the air, although it's a little fishy-smelling where the refuse gathers. And there, lying in a few inches of water, wet and very still, was a little baby.

I couldn't even believe it.

His skin was brown and sunburned, his hair was dark and plastered to his head, and his eyes were closed. I thought he was dead at first. I figured some immigrant family lost him trying to cross the river, and I wondered if any of them had survived. My heart broke to think the little baby hadn't.

And then like a miracle, just like the sun breaking the horizon, he opened his eyes and looked right at me. I was so surprised I fell over backwards in the shallows. But then I scrambled to him, because he was still in the water, too. I gathered him up and took him back to my little tent, talking soft to him the whole time.

He didn't cry. I know all about babies. I've been babysitting for two years—three different newborns, too. So I knew this baby's quiet wasn't the good kind. He ought to be crying.

I rifled through my stuff, found the sunburn ointment I'd swiped from some careless campers—I'm a pale-skinned, green-eyed redhead from the southern tier of New York state. The Texas sun is not my friend. So I dabbed it on his little nose, cheeks, and forehead and on the red patches on his arms and chubby thighs.

He wore a dirty white baby T-shirt with snaps between the legs that were unsnapped. His diaper was long gone, and that was probably a good thing. It might've dragged him under.

He still didn't cry as I fussed with him. I took off his wet T-shirt. He had a bracelet tied around his wrist, snug but not tight. Braided leather, I thought, with a beaded border, and the word "WOLF" spelled out in beads. The letter O was a white stone engraved with a wolf's head, tipped back, howling.

I washed the river water off him, then wrapped him in my soft blanket. Still, he didn't cry. He didn't gurgle or coo either. I thought he might be too weak or sick. I thought about taking him to a hospital, but I've heard awful things about what happens to immigrant children when they're caught by authorities.

I remembered that there was a couple with a new baby in a big fancy camper out on the road that led to the pool. I didn't want to leave my baby alone, but I figured he'd been alone for a while now. He'd be okay for a few more minutes. Heck, he was okay on the river all by himself. Somehow. He could handle another few minutes bundled, warm, dry, and safe.

He closed his eyes again, maybe went to sleep. I hoped so. His little chest moved up and down rapidly, and I didn't know if that was normal. But he didn't have a fever and wasn't wheezing or coughing or anything.

When I left, I zipped the tent up tight and prayed he wouldn't wake and cry and call in a big cat or a coyote or a bear or whatever might be out there. All I've seen so far are scrawny red deer, and a few skinny rabbits or hares, I guess, down here. New York wildlife were way fatter. There could be anything out there, for all I know. I've only been in Texas for a few weeks now.

I told myself to be fast and smart, hopped on my bike, and rode straight to the site where the big camper was parked. It had two sliders, fully extended, and was lit up like a castle.

I skidded to a halt on the narrow lane, inches beyond the pool of light their camper spread, just as the couple came out together. The dad carried the baby, and the mom carried a huge diaper bag over her shoulder. She walked to the car, put the bag into the trunk, and left it open. The dad leaned into the car to put the baby into its car seat and began fussing with the buckles.

I saw my moment. I didn't sneak. I ran to that open trunk, snatched the diaper bag, and raced back to my bike. I didn't know if anyone saw me or not. I just picked up my bike and took off, pedaling like mad.

No one shouted or came running after me.

I sped all the way back to the baby. The whole trip took around ten minutes.

That diaper bag turned out to be a pure treasure! Bottles, baby clothes, diapers, cans of formula with pop tops and instructions, thank goodness, and three hundred dollars in cash.

I took one of the bottles, filled it from a can as instructed, didn't bother warming it, as room-temperature down here was pretty warm. Cradling the baby in my arms, I held the bottle to his lips.

He didn't react at first, but I tapped his lips with the nipple, like I'd had to do for the Hutchinsons' preemie. I moved it back and forth across his pouty little mouth. He tried to grab on. I squeezed a little formula out for him, and that seemed to light his fuse. He latched on and sucked two ounces down. He slept a little, and then woke up just now, and I fed him some more. He downed more this time, and now he's sleeping again.

I curled up beside him and slept for a little while, too.

And then just a little while ago, he woke me up with strong, healthy crying that sounded like a baby's supposed to sound. I'm pretty sure he's going to be okay.

"Hi, little guy," I said. "I'm Cilla."

He's looking up at me right now, from huge brown eyes with lighter brown streaks. They remind me of the tiger's eye stone on my dresser back home. I swear he's telling me something with those eyes.

I'm going to keep this baby. He was a gift from the river. He's mine. I've been all by myself, barely even exchanging words with strangers. But he was sent to me, somehow. I feel like I was meant to find him.

I'm holding his little hand, looking at that bracelet as he wraps his fingers around mine. The moonstone just caught a sun ray and reflected a pearlescent rainbow at me. That bracelet is his only possession from his life before the river. I want to make sure he'll always have a part of himself, but the bracelet might fall apart or get lost. So I'm going to call him Wolf. That way, no matter what else happens, he'll always have his name.

CAMELLIA

"I can't read anymore," Camellia said. "My eyes are too wet."

"Same," Wolf admitted. He was still driving. She'd been reading from the diary for a while. "Let's take a break, huh?" He reached for the radio dial, but only turned it on low. Soft country music cushioned the space between them.

"Yeah. How much further?"

"Another five hours, give or take."

"We'll *definitely* need another meal."

"Yeah, and to figure out what we're doing when we get there," he said. "It's a national park. We don't have a reservation."

"Oh, I know. I did some checking earlier. There won't be internet or cell service down there, and they don't have cabins to rent."

"There a motel nearby?"

She liked how he said motel. With the accent on the *mo*. "No, but there are campsites available."

He glanced her way, then at the road, then at her again. "I haven't been camping since I was four."

"I have. Dad used to take us. That gigantic duffle in the back. That's our gear."

"Oh," he said. "I thought you were just a heavy packer."

She laughed a little bit, wishing she could've heard his thoughts when she'd thrown that four-foot-long duffel into the truck bed. And yet he hadn't said a word.

"Dad was always so proud he could get everything we needed into one large bag." She shrugged a shoulder at him, like a challenge. "We can stop along the way for anything else we might need. Fresh batteries, a couple of tanks of propane, some food and water."

"You've thought this through."

"Like I said, I didn't sleep last night."

He nodded, was quiet for a moment, but she could feel him working up to something. Eventually he said, "Do you really think this ex of yours—?"

"Earl," she said. "Stafford."

"You really think he's capable of violence?"

He was asking if Earl had ever hit her without asking if he'd ever hit her. She said, "I wouldn't have been so scared of him if I didn't think he was capable of violence. I even bought a gun." And it was in her bag, and nobody but her needed to know about that. "He never hurt me, but he was getting more… I want to say radicalized, you know, against a lot of things, but mainly women. And I started feeling like I wasn't safe around him. Like it was progressing. Right before we split, he shoved me once when I defended a woman he was griping about, a congresswoman. He shoved me so hard, I fell on the floor. So that seems like progression to me. And now, the girlfriend."

"Yeah."

"It has me shaken, I admit it. I mean, a few miles ago I saw a big black Blazer just like he used to drive pulling into a rest area. My heart liked to pound right through my chest."

He looked at her hard. "Was it his?"

"Different plate number." She lowered her head, blew out a sigh. "Sorry. I got off topic. So? Are you up for camping?"

"I guess I'm up for camping," he said. But he was looking at her with a combination of concern and ferocity in his gorgeous eyes.

"Cool. I'll reserve us a spot." She tapped her phone as an excuse not to gaze into those tiger's eyes for too long. Then she got genuinely distracted. "There's a site open near the river!" And then she tapped again.

DREW BRAND, TEXAS BRAND RANCH, QUINN COUNTY, TEXAS

"I don't know for sure how Willow's doing with all this," Drew said. They'd gathered outside the bunkhouse at the Texas Brand ranch. Elena happened to be the one standing closest. She was the newest member of the clan, a step-cousin, not a blood relative, but being a Brand was a matter of heart and character more than blood. Elena was their adopted cousin Ethan's half-sister—they shared a birth father and not one drop of Brand blood—and she was a doctor at the only medical clinic in the town of Quinn and one of only three in Quinn county. "Help me keep an eye on her?"

"Sure," Elena said. "Anything in particular you're worried about?"

"She's tense as a bowstring," Drew replied. "I just keep worrying she'll snap or something, like her mom apparently did twenty-eight years ago. I already spoke to Maria and Lily, so I figure between us she-Brands, we've got her back." Then she frowned. "What? You're looking at me funny."

Elena gave her head a shake. "I just... Do you know how special it is, what you all have? This family?"

"What *we* all have, Elena. We. And you know what? I appreciate the reminder, 'cause I'm so used to it, I forget. I get irritated sometimes with the way everybody knows everybody's business, and nobody hesitates to offer passionate opinions on anybody else's life choices. But we do pull together in times of trouble. And we put on a mean barbecue."

"The two keys to family unity," Elena said.

"You're handling it all great, for an only child."

"I always wanted a great big family." Elena shrugged. "Kids always want what they don't have, I guess."

"Well, you got your wish. Come on, everyone's here."

The cousins had all gathered at the bunkhouse, a meadow

removed from the main house on the Texas Brand ranch. All, that was, except for Willow, who was late.

But Willow already knew the plan. She had dictated the terms and assigned Drew to put it all together.

"Okay," Drew said. "So Willow wants a road trip down near Big Bend, where our baby cousin's blanket was found tangled on a limb in the Rio Grande. And she put me in charge, so you have to do what I say."

"Willow put the littlest cousin in charge?" Ethan asked, pushing his hat back on his head. He towered over Drew like a mountain over a pebble. "Welp, I'd interpret being *in charge* as you scoping out the route and food stops. Tell me, little cousin, what did you do instead?"

She pushed up her chin. "I booked us a river ride. We'll be in canoes, with guides, and they'll take us right to the spot where the blanket was found. Uncle Wes remembers it exactly. He and Uncle Garrett went there, I guess." She stopped and lowered her head, wishing Willow would get there, so she could quit worrying. "But they only had three canoes available, so there's only room for six of us, two to a canoe with a guide in each."

"Lily's too pregnant for a river ride," Ethan said in his deep voice. "And I don't much like leavin' her."

"You're going," Lily told her husband. "You have to go. I'll be fine here at home for an afternoon."

"I'll stay behind, too," Elena said. "I can't leave the clinic without backup. Even on my day off, I can't be that many hours away." Then she smiled over at Lily. "I'll keep a good eye on your bride, Ethan."

A dust cloud appeared in the distance and Drew felt a little better. "Willow said Jeremiah's staying behind with Frankie and the dog," she told the others, "so that leaves me, Orrin, Trevor, Maria-Michelle, Baxter, Ethan, and Willow. Still one too many."

"We'll make room," Ethan said. "Drew, you're so little, you can sit on my knee."

Everyone chuckled. Drew seethed. She hated being the littlest Brand. Nobody took her seriously.

"We'll drive four hours," she said. "That's where the outfitter is. Then we take the river the rest of the way. It's all booked and you owe me seventy-five bucks apiece. And," she said, pointing to the growing dust cloud, "I rented a van to keep our energy use down."

A few of the guys groaned as the van rolled closer. Willow was driving. The van was sleek, aerodynamic, and green, both literally—deep olive with a glossy shine—and figuratively—it was a hybrid.

Willow got out with a cardboard trayful of takeout coffees with lids, each marked with initials. She handed one to each of the cousins as they piled into the van. Maria hugged her nerdy husband, Harrison, way longer than Drew thought a daytrip called for, and Ethan had a hell of a time tearing himself away from Lily and her swollen belly, though she kept swearing she'd be fine.

Eventually, though, they were off. Willow drove and Ethan was co-pilot—mainly because his long legs needed the extra leg room up front.

Baxter, Orrin, and Trevor took up the third-row seat, leaving Drew and Maria-Michelle in the middle.

Several hours and one rest stop later, they were wearing yellow life vests and stepping into beautiful wooden canoes, two in each with a guide in between. Trev and Orrin paired up. Maria, Drew, and Willow got into a single boat, and Drew convinced the guides they were small enough to make it work. The female guide, Lupe, also the smallest of her crew, agreed and got in with them. Baxter shared a canoe with Ethan and the other male guide—dwarfing the poor guy.

They pushed off in a beautiful spot where you could see forever, and the current carried them easily. Soon the stone through which the river had cut for centuries rose ever higher, until they were floating between stone canyons 1500 feet tall.

"This is stunning," Drew said.

"How's your mom doing, Willow?" Maria asked. She'd tucked her wild red curls into a baseball cap. They were doing their best to escape.

"She hasn't talked to anybody," Willow said. "Not even Aunt Chelsea. Racked with guilt still."

"Yeah. I can't even imagine what she's been through," Drew said. "Or you either, for that matter." Willow was the only one without a paddle. Drew had one in front, for steering, and Maria in the rear for power. They had to coordinate, paddling on opposite sides. The guide had a paddle "just in case." But Drew thought she and Maria-Michelle were killing it.

Willow said, "This part is kind of beautiful. And I have to admit it's nice to get away."

"Your destination's just around this bend," their guide, Lupe, said. She was pretty and she obviously loved her work. She hadn't stopped smiling since they'd pushed off.

"Follow the other boats," she said.

They paddled their canoes into the corner between a tributary and the mother river. Further ahead, whitecaps appeared, and the river narrowed. "Rapids up ahead," the guide in one of the other boats called as he dipped his paddle to help Baxter and Ethan steer their canoe in.

Soon all three gleaming wooden canoes were lined up on the bank, and the cousins and guides were standing around in a wild and untamed spot. There were scrubby bushes around, and disappointingly, she could see litter in the still water of a smaller branch up a little ways, collecting in the shallows. The tall stone cliffs had given way to more level ground, with trees, red-brown dirt, and boulders. Taller rock formations stood like soldiers in the background.

"This is the spot?" Drew asked Lupe.

"This is the spot you described, yes," she said. "You said something was found near here? That would make sense, as the current dumps refuse near here all the time." She nodded at the spot a little further upriver. Its shore was brushy, no clear finger of ground like there was here.

"They say the river takes its garbage out here," said one of the other guides.

Drew winced a little at that description and sent a worried look at Willow.

"Even if he somehow survived this far," Willow said softly, giving voice to what they were all thinking, "he couldn't have made it much farther." She looked at where the water became raging white-water rapids, with boulders winking in and out of the depths.

"What's out here?" Drew asked, looking inland.

"Big Bend National Park."

Drew looked at Willow, and their eyes held for a moment before Will gave her a subtle nod. This was the spot then. "If you guides could give us some privacy?" Drew said, "I'll text you when we're ready to move on."

"No signal," Lupe said. "We can come back in twenty minutes. Is that enough time?"

Again, Drew looked at Willow, who already had tears in her eyes. Then she said, "Twenty minutes should be fine," in a gruff voice.

"Okay. See you in a little while." The guides peeled away from the little group of cousins. Drew watched as Willow opened her backpack and took out a small pouche, a bundle of herbs, a lighter, and an eagle feather.

WOLF, BIG BEND NATIONAL PARK

Wolf steered the pickup through the campground's entrance. They'd stopped off at a grocery store nearby, where everything was overpriced, and got a few supplies—boil-in-the-bag meals and drinking water among them.

They drove up to the gatehouse, and a uniformed woman with curly orange hair and a friendly smile said, "Welcome to Big Bend. Can I see your reservation?"

Camellia passed her phone to Wolf, and he held it out the window. "Oh, nice spot. You'll have a view of the river from there."

"I thought it was *on* the river," Camellia said. She leaned across Wolf to say it, and his hand rose without his permission. He stopped it halfway to stroking her hair. What the hell kind of an impulse was that? They were *friends*. He'd *promised*. She was afraid of men, thanks to Earl. One false move on his part, and she'd tell him to hit the road. Even now, she didn't trust him. Not really. He recognized it, because he'd been raised by a woman who trusted no one, and he trusted very few people himself.

Camellia and her mom were a rare exception to that. He wasn't sure why. He hadn't decided to trust them; he just did. It was a gut-level thing.

And not the only one. The more he was around Camellia, the more he wanted to be around her.

"Mmm, it's *sort of* on the river," the ranger said. "Great site though, as long as neither of you sleepwalk." She laughed softly as she handed a one-sheet map out the window. "I marked your route."

"Thank you, um, Sally," Wolf said with a quick glance at the ranger's name badge. He took the map and passed it to Camellia, who'd returned to her own side of the car. Sadly.

Stop it.

"You have a great stay, folks." Ranger Sally waved them

through the open gate. He drove slowly over the paved paths, following directions to a parking area with a sign: "No motor vehicles beyond this point."

"Guess we walk from here," Wolf said as he parked the truck.

"We'll have to reconfigure our things a little," Camellia said, hopping out.

She had a bounce in her step as she went around behind the pickup and climbed right up into its bed. Then she found a seat and unzipped the gigantic duffel. "There's room for some of the food we picked up in here, and we can stuff the rest into our backpacks. Here, hand me one of those grocery bags from up front."

He did, and then watched as she fit things into the packs like she was playing Tetris. She moved the soft items—bread and chips and the like—into their smaller packs, the ones that held their clothes, and zipped them in with care.

"That should do it," she said, passing his backpack over the side. "We can take turns carrying the big one. She pulled her own bag's strap over her shoulders, then hopped out of the truck again, reaching back for the larger one.

He beat her to it. It wasn't all that heavy, which surprised him since she'd said it had "everything they'd need." He hoped she was right.

He locked the truck, then followed her. She'd spotted a wooden stand, covered to protect it from the weather, with a book on a chain, and several pens in a cup. "SIGN IN STATION: TENT CAMPING."

Beside the station, there was a faucet labeled "potable water." He paused to fish his empty canteen out of his pack and filled it. "Hand me yours," he said. "Save our bottles for when we need them."

Camellia did, and he filled it, then passed it back to her. "There should be another tap near our site," she said, pointing at one of the smiling blue droplet symbols that dotted the map.

She wrote her name in the sign-in book and passed him the pen.

He leaned in, wrote his first name, then stopped with the pen hovering over the page.

Camellia said, "Your last name doesn't feel real to you right now, does it?"

"Trouble," he said. "It's just a fancy word for trouble. At least my first name means something." He lifted up his arm as he said it, and he saw her notice the bracelet there.

"Wait...is that the bracelet from Cilla's journal?" He nodded. "How?" she asked. "It was so tiny!"

"A Native fellow had a stand outside the gas station the other day. Looked to be a hundred years old. Said his name was Turtle."

She repeated the name softly.

"He was selling jewelry. I got the notion to show it to him. Well, that old man took it right outta my hand and started picking its strands apart. Then he grabbed a couple lengths of cord and somehow wove them into what was already there." He turned his wrist slowly, showing off the intricate braids and knots, then twisted it back to the moonstone with the wolf head engraving. "Wolf means something to me. It was attached to me when the river spat me out."

"Oh, no, that's not what the river did," Camellia said. "The river gave birth to you. Your second birth."

He didn't meet her eyes, but her words touched him so much his throat got tight. She had a perspective that was lighter than his, more positively focused.

He was still staring at where he'd written his name in the book.

"Even without a real surname, you know who you are."

"An Indian who's never gone camping?" he asked, meeting her eyes at last. "Native American, I mean."

"I think you get to say Indian if you want to."

He lowered his head. "I don't even know what tribe or clan or anything about my people."

"We're going to find out, Wolf. We've barely got started."

"You really think there's anything here to find?" He looked around, like there would be an answer out there amid the scrub brush and boulders.

"You know what?" she asked. "Just leave your last name off. And when we find your origin story, we'll come back here and you can write it in then. Now let's get a move on, so we can set up camp before dark."

He nodded and put the pen down. "I like the idea of coming back here to write my real name, if we find it."

"When we find it."

CHAPTER SEVEN

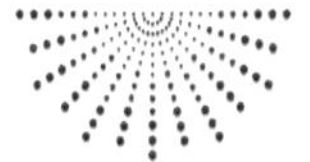

WOLF

olf had got to know Camellia better on the long drive down. She was a natural optimist, but he thought the phone call from her ex had let some of the air out of her balloon.

The further he'd driven, the more her buoyancy had returned, though. She walked briskly, with a bounce in her step. He liked her. It felt good being around her.

The landscape held more boulders than trees. Rock formations that protruded from shrub-scattered patches of all but barren ground seemed to rise higher the farther they hiked. They'd passed a fork in the trail, where the other way had veered downhill. Their route went up. There was a water spigot right at the fork, the last one before their site, according to the colorful map.

The air was hot and dry, and it smelled different than the air back home. Something inside Wolf drank it in, and he wondered if his lungs remembered it from when he'd been a baby. It felt that way. There was a sense of relief, like a weight rising from him. What was that?

Maybe it was because his ancestors had come from here.

"Whoa," Camellia said. She'd stopped in the trail. He walked up beside her and stopped as well.

They were at the top of a cliff, with a sheer drop to the river far below. Across from them stood an equally high cliff. The river had split the stone, and its face was an earth-tone rainbow, with stripes of red and brown and black and tan, and bits that sparkled when viewed from certain angles.

Camellia moved closer to him and clasped his upper arm in her hand. "This is just…wow. How far down is the river, do you think?"

"A thousand feet?"

"Look how small those people are!" She pointed.

Far below, at a spot where a strand split off from the river, a group of people had gathered. One of them held something that wafted smoke.

"It's some kind of ceremony," Camellia whispered. "She looks Native." And just as she said it, the woman far below paused and looked up, right at Wolf.

He raised his hand, and she raised hers back.

And then she bent near the water's edge and the smoke stopped. When she rose, everyone in the group hugged her and each other. Then they got into some waiting canoes and floated around the bend into the faster moving waters.

He watched them until the last canoe was out of sight.

Camellia squeezed his arm. "Wolf, this was a really good sign."

"Maybe it was," he said. Then he turned her way "But I don't want to camp up here. What do you say we look for a site down below, near the river?"

She pulled out her phone, tapped it several times, and shook her head. "No signal. I can't book a different site, or even see which ones are taken."

"If somebody shows up, we'll just say we read our map wrong, apologize, and move on," he said. "No harm done. I really want to go down there—near where those folks were. Let's head back to the split and take the righthand fork this time."

"You got it." She reached for the bigger bag. "My turn to carry this for a while. Especially since we're heading *down*hill." She slung it over her shoulder and trudged off ahead of him.

WILLOW, BIG BEND NATIONAL PARK

Willow had braided sage and sweet grass into a thick bunch that produced ribbons of fragrant smoke when it burned. She'd held it up in honor of her ancestors, as she whispered a plea for their help in finding out what had happened to her brother. As the smoke rose and twisted, she turned to each of the four winds, repeating her gestures and words.

The air had been still, but a brisk gust swept down the cliff faces and rode the river, buffeting them all. She was facing west, lifting her gaze and her smudge bundle as one.

At the top of a cliff stood a man. He had long black hair, blown by the wind, very much like her own. He raised a hand. She started to raise hers, then a burst of wind threw red dust into her eyes, and she had to squeeze them tight and cover her face. She knelt to extinguish the burning smudge and splashed some river water into her eyes to rinse the grit away.

When she looked again, the light had shifted, and man was no longer in her sight.

"I think my brother *must* be dead," she whispered so softly only Drew could hear.

"Why?" Drew whispered back, her blue eyes wide and round.

Drew had been sticking super close to Willow since she'd

learned about her lost sibling. Willow knew her littlest cousin was trying to play big sister, and it touched her. "I think I just saw his spirit."

Drew frowned. "You mean that guy who was standing up on the cliff?"

"You saw him, too?" Willow asked.

"Sure, I did. That was no spirit. That was just a hiker, taking in the view. It's a national park, Will." She put her hands on Willow's shoulders. "Are you okay?"

Willow looked up at the cliff again, then sighed and nodded. "Yeah, I'm okay. I'm glad we did this."

The guides came back, and it was time to go. They all got back into their canoes, and as they paddled away from shore, Willow felt oddly reluctant to leave. She kept looking back through tears. Her cousins were *all* watching her now, not just Drew. The family was worried.

As they rounded a gentle bend, she could see how rough and fast the water became up ahead. They were going to ride the small stretch of rapids. The shuttles to take them back to their van would be waiting on the other side.

As she looked at the white water, she thought that even if her brother had survived this far, he wouldn't have made it any farther.

"Shoot, my phone!" Maria-Michelle cried.

Willow turned to see her cousin's phone bounding away from her in its plastic zipper bag. "I need that phone!" she cried.

She wasn't being dramatic. She was the town vet. Her being without her phone was not an option. Being the Brand man nearest, Baxter sprang into action, bracing his arms on the sides of his canoe and vaulting over the side into the water. He let out a hoot, so it must've been cold, sank out of sight, but then popped up again.

The water rushing past him was neck deep, and he was dang

near as tall as Ethan. Still, he half-swam, half-waded toward the phone.

The phone, however, was faster.

"It's not going far!" the guide from the boat they shared said.

Everyone angled their boats into a small strand that split off from the side of the river, and Baxter continued wading into the calmer shallows.

"See?" the guide called.

Sure enough, the air-filled baggy floated straight into that gathering of garbage on the shore. There were pieces of clothing, a shoe, a backpack with its straps torn off, multiple beer and pop cans, and dozens of other things.

"Everything that doesn't sink winds up here," said Graham, the guide between Trevor and Orrin.

Willow sat in her canoe, which was resting in the shallow inlet, and stared at the pile of garbage in the water along the shore. "This must be where they found the blanket," she whispered on tight vocal cords. "Maybe the baby washed up here, too."

"*Baby?*" Lupe sounded so stunned it made Willow turn to look at her. Her eyes were round and horrified.

"I'm—"

"Writing a screenplay," Drew filled in.

Willow said, "Yeah. Writing a screenplay." What a joke. She could barely stand to write arrest reports. Then she looked at her cousins all around her, and for a second just appreciated that they *were* all around her. Each acknowledged in silence that they'd heard the lie and would support it. "A baby gets swept away in a flash-flood, and somehow, survives."

"Right," said Trevor. "So the first bit of research is to find out how that could've happened and whether it's even possible. Right, Willow?"

"Exactly, Trevor."

"I thought you were a police officer." The guide was

concerned. She probably feared she was aiding and abetting some baby-dumping ring.

"Deputy sheriff." *Not the same thing.* "The writing is…a—"

"Side gig," said Drew.

The guide frowned, looking at her colleagues as Baxter grabbed the phone and waded back to the boat. He handed it up to Maria-Michelle, then climbed back in his own canoe, while Ethan and their guide Matt kept it upright.

"Thanks," Maria said. "But now you're soaked."

"He'll be okay," Lupe said. "It's only another twenty minutes to the van. You all ready?"

Everyone looked at Willow, including Baxter, who was soaking wet. "Let's go then."

The current picked up, and then the roar of the water got too loud for conversation as the cousins were swept into the rapids.

WOLF

Wolf gathered wood for a small fire, and Camellia laid it up over dried grasses and weeds and lit it with a lighter. Fires were forbidden in the park at certain times of the year, but not just then.

The fire licked at the dried-out driftwood they'd gathered along the river's edge, where they'd pitched their tent. Wolf settled into the squatty camp chair beside it. The thing was canvas with a wooden frame, its legs were only six inches long, and it folded smaller than your average umbrella. There'd been two of them in Camellia's "everything we'll need" bag.

There was a tiny village with a few more amenities nearby. They'd hiked out to a diner there to grab sandwiches for their dinner.

His beautiful companion was sitting in another chair beside him, her long legs stretched out in front of her, crossed at the ankles. He liked the way the fire lit her eyes and told himself he shouldn't.

At least she was starting to relax a little bit. Maybe because there'd been no further sign of Earl or his Blazer, and because they were far from Hobbsville. He thought she felt safe. And that might be partly because he'd kept his feelings to himself and she was starting to trust him.

His feelings, however, were changing rapidly. Or maybe they were just coming more fully online as he gained distance from the death of his mother and the shock of her revelations. His attraction to Camellia was powerful, but there was more. Something beyond the physical.

Yeah, the kind of stuff I don't believe in.

He shook his head at his own bizarre train of thought.

They'd waited to get "home" before eating their dinner of sandwiches and potato chips, and she was still working on hers. He kept looking at her while trying not to let on that he was. He liked looking at her. And he still hadn't seen her with her hair down.

She did seem more relaxed, he thought. Maybe he could... broach the subject of...them. The thing was, it was becoming clearer and clearer to Wolf that he didn't want to be Camellia's friend. He wanted to be her lover.

Even as he thought it, she reached across the space between his chair and hers and clasped his hand. His heart sped up. Hell, maybe her feelings were changing, too.

She said, "I want to thank you, Wolf."

He turned his hand over so they were palm to palm. Her hand felt good there, small and warm, with their fingers sliding between each other's. "For what? You're the one helping me here."

"It's helping me, too. I feel safe with you. And I wouldn't have if you'd been all…but you haven't. You haven't been like that at all. You've been a gentleman. It's good to know they still exist."

Ice water dousing complete.

Wolf gave her hand a squeeze, then let it go and took his beer from his camping chair's cup holder. He took a big enough drink to relax his loins. He liked Camellia. Her trust in him made him feel pretty damn good, and it also made him feel like he didn't want to break it. She felt safe with him. That made him feel ten feet tall. He couldn't let on that he was just a horn-dog who wanted to get into her pants, like every other guy she knew.

She was absolutely irresistible. Of course every guy she knew wanted her.

He said, "I'm beyond sorry he scared you so much."

"He didn't at first. Like I said, he changed. Got in with a group of fanatics. Gun club, ostensibly. But it got progressively darker, meaner. He was always talking about everything he was against—which was dang near everything—and how society was better when women stayed home and raised the kids." She lowered her head, shaking it. "I knew it was over before I ended it. That last day, he was pissed I wouldn't let him use my dad's camping gear for one of his angry-boy campouts."

"You wouldn't let him use it?" Wolf asked, raising his brows.

"Hell, no. He wasn't worthy of my dad's stuff."

He couldn't help himself. "Does that mean…you think I am?" he asked. Shit, was that flirting? That was definitely flirting. He wanted to pull the words back.

She shrugged one shoulder and said, "Most worthy, I think." And she tapped her bottle to his and took a slug. "Earl wasn't, though. He hated everyone. Immigrants, gays, women." She shrugged. "I noticed the last few times we went out that he brought a gun along. On a date. Can you *even*?"

"I can't *even*," he agreed.

"But that last day, he shoved me, and I fell, and I realized the guy's a lot bigger than me and decided to stop waiting for the right moment to end it. It was clear he was getting worse, not better."

The fire snapped loud and shot red sparks into the night sky. They faded to black on the way back down.

"After we broke up, I saw him in that black Blazer of his a couple of times, parked near where I was working a case. Once I started paying attention, I realized he was following me. Then the calls started, and the creepy gifts arrived at my work or at my mom's house."

"Creepy gifts?"

"A ball-gag, a vibrator, whips, paddles, shit like that."

Wolf swore softly.

"Threatening notes too, talking about how he'd teach me to be a good girlfriend this time."

He swore louder.

"I called the cops. Detective Marcia Simms had me start documenting everything. So I did. He was brought in, questioned, lectured. We were gathering evidence for a restraining order when he just…" She raised her open hands. "Stopped. I assumed the cops talking to him shook him, you know? But no, turns out that's right around the time he changed his status from 'it's complicated' to 'in a relationship' and tagged that poor girl who's now dead."

She closed her eyes. "Mary Jo Gallagher."

"You're safe here, though," Wolf said, because he could see that talking about Earl brought the tension back to Camellia's face, to her eyes, to her body. She was all tight and trembling again.

"I feel safe," she said. "But I need a little distraction."

He could use a little distraction, too, but she probably wasn't thinking of the same kind he was. She went into the tent and came right back out with his mother's diary. "Shall we read?"

That would probably do it. "Okay, but it's my turn," he said, holding out a hand.

She handed him the old journal. He opened to where they'd

left off on the drive, cleared his throat, and said, "Wow, she took a long break. This section was a few months later later."

CILLA

January 15th

Our lives changed entirely today. I need to get this down while it's all fresh in my mind, for Wolf.

He's four months old, near as I can figure. He has sleek black hair and skin like the red rocks that rise among the more common brown ones. The older he gets, the prettier he gets.

We've been venturing farther into the rocky badlands from the park, way up into the tops of those towering cliffs above the Rio Grande, and then farther from the river, among the boulders. I carry Wolf in the backpack-baby carrier I made from his diaper bag. I didn't know what we were looking for until today when we found it.

A tumble-down shack with a rock formation behind it that looks like an anvil balanced on top of a pole—like it's just waiting for Wile E. Coyote to pass by so it can fall on his head and flatten him. It's up high, and it smells good there. Even better than below. There's no fishy smell from the river, and the warm, dry wind comes fresh from the sky, and isn't yet contaminated with all the nonsense down below.

The outside of the shack is made of wide boards that have more splinters than a porcupine has quills, sun-bleached to palest gray. There are two windows in the front, covered from within. A crooked chimney of cobblestones is the most solid-looking part of the whole building. Outside, there's a tiny, falling-down barn, a well with a hand-pump, and patches of weeds that look more or less cultivated. The place looks abandoned, but not.

It looks as if it wants to look abandoned.

Okay, I'm writing this as closely as I can to how it happened.

Wolf chattered like I'd never heard him before as we got closer. The shack didn't feel empty. It felt...sad. Lonely. From a few feet outside the door, hanging crooked with one hinge loose, I called, "Hello?"

No one replied, so I moved closer and said it again. "Hello? Is anyone there?"

"Please." Her voice was soft and hoarse. It came from inside the shack.

I went to the door, but hesitated. I had to think of the baby, after all. What if this was some kind of criminal, holed up out here in the middle of nowhere, luring us in to...rob us, or whatever?

"I need water."

That was definitely a woman's voice. I was sure of it. An old woman, I thought, and I opened the door just a little bit, so I could get a look inside.

An old Black woman lay in a bed inside the house, over near the front window to the left of the door. She had pure white hair like a ripe dandelion and skin of faded leather. Her fireplace was cold and dark. Herbs hung upside down in bundles from the ceiling.

She said, "There you are," in a raspy voice and asked for water.

I looked around the place to make sure nobody was waiting to jump me before going inside. But the shack was empty. So I grabbed the pitcher and ran back out, then started pumping the well handle up and down.

At first nothing came out of the well's spout, and I was afraid it had gone dry. But then I heard an encouraging gurgle, and after more pumping, water gushed out. It hit the pitcher so hard it rebounded back up into my face, and I sputtered.

Then I realized I was thirsty, too, and this water was sweet. I pumped a few times till it ran clear, then rinsed the dust from the pitcher and filled it. I took a sip as I hurried back inside, where I quickly rinsed and then filled the glass.

Standing beside the bed with Wolf on my back, I held it out.

The old woman lifted her head and reached out weakly. Then she let her hand fall to the mattress beside her, and her head sank back onto her pillow. So I knelt beside the bed and held the glass to her lips. She drank deeply and when I started to move the glass away, she put a hand over mine to hold it there longer and drank more.

Finally, she relaxed back. I told her I wasn't whoever she was expecting, but she said we were exactly who she'd been expecting and asked me to show her the baby.

I was protective of Wolf, but I did not think this woman was a threat.

I slid the carrier from my shoulders, eased the baby out of it, and went to the edge of the bed to give the old woman a closer look. She was probably senile, and apparently all alone out here.

Then she said, "You're the one. I had a vision you'd come."

And when I looked skeptical, she told me when death is near, visions come strong. A white girl with a Comanche child from the river came to her in this vision. The girl told her she would care for her until her death in exchange for a safe place to raise the child.

I looked more closely at her face, my inborn skepticism rising. Mom got so mad when we all went to see a magic show, and I spent the whole time trying to explain how the magician did the tricks.

But the old woman knew he came from the river. How could that be? I asked her what else she knew. What would become of us, Wolf and me?

The old woman waved a hand. She said something like, "I only saw what I saw. You came. You stayed. It was good. Isn't that enough for right now?"

I thought about it, certain the woman wasn't up to anything nefarious, but also sure she was a little bit crazy. Still, this place is way better than our tent.

She frowned, then refilled the water glass herself, drank it down, and nodded. She offered to hold the baby and talk me through making us all some dinner.

So I placed the baby into her frail arms, noting that if she dropped him, he'd only roll onto her mattress and blankets.

Oh, the look that came into her brown eyes then was something else. Bliss, maybe. I haven't really given a crap about another person for a long time, other than Wolf. Even before I left home... I loved my mom, but it always felt like I was loving her from behind an invisible wall. There was always this barrier between us. Between me and everyone. It was made by the secret I had to keep. I knew that much.

But there was no such barrier between me and my baby.

And as the old woman held him close, after he was warm and fed and content, something moved inside my heart. At that very moment, her old brown eyes shifted, took hold of mine and held, and held. She said all that happened to me had brought me there. And that this was a good place. Then she said her name was Sage.

I know it's her chosen name, not her given one. I don't know how I know it—I just do. I went through her cabinets and searched among the barrels where dried beans and grains were stored. Sage held the baby and called out instructions. Fetch in wood and kindle the fire. Take the bigger pitcher to the pump and bring back water to pour into the pot. Swing the arm, pot and all, over the fire and put the lid on to keep the ashes out. Then prepare the vegetables.

She had potatoes, carrots, and onions in bins or hanging from the ceiling in braids. I added beans and some of the barley. There's a lot of food stashed in this place.

After the veggies and grains, I added herbs, plucking from bunches Sage pointed out, her namesake, and rosemary and thyme. She told me how to grate a turmeric root over the pot, then I ground black pepper right on top and gave the blend a stir. The most important ingredient, Sage told me, remained. But I'd have to go out back to get it.

I hesitated, unsure about leaving her alone with Wolf, but he seemed more content with her than I'd ever seen him. He was patting her face and babbling his life story. So I went out past the Wile E. Coyote rock. There were shaded beds in trenches two or more feet deep. Pots of greens lined them. They had pallets propped on either side, leaning against each other, forming a roof-shaped shelter over the plants, but looking like a pile of junk from a distance. The pallets were slatted, but they still reduced the amount of sun on the green leaves.

There were various types of greens in pots. I crawled along on hands and knees, using the plant shears Sage had lent me to snip a few leaves from each type of plant.

I filled the bowl, squished the contents down, and filled it again, repeating this until I couldn't get any more in. Then, as instructed, I rinsed the greens at the well, shook them dry, brought them inside, and dumped them into the pot.

I stirred the stew, then went to take the baby from the old woman.

Her eyes met mine, and her smile stayed in place. She let me see how welcome we were and how happy she was to have us, and it felt so good. I can't explain it.

Well, Wolf fell asleep in her arms.

She already looks far better than she did when we arrived at her doorstep. Maybe she was mostly just thirsty, hungry, and lonely.

Sage nodded toward a corner, where a burlap sack covered a shape.

I went over there and pulled the sack away. There was a wooden cradle with a still shrink-wrapped baby mattress inside, brand-new.

I was stunned and shot her my questions with my eyes.

I asked why she had the cradle, a little of my natural suspicion coming back.

Sage was busy untangling her white hair from the baby's fist. He'd fallen asleep with a handful and didn't seem inclined to let go.

She told me how she gets by, selling and trading her herbs, plants, and paintings at a local flea market every weekend. She'd traded for the cradle and mattress after that vision she'd had. She said with my help, we could grow more herbs—enough for formula and diapers and vaccines, all the things a baby needs.

I blinked. I could hardly believe what she was saying and asked her if she really meant it. That she wanted us to stay.

She nodded and sank back down onto her bed again, probably exhausted after being so sick and immobile. She said her bedroom used to be the loft, until it got too hard for her to go up and down the ladder. Said it could be mine now—that a young woman needed some privacy.

Then she added that before I made up my mind I should know, she'd *decided not to die just yet. I smiled at her. I couldn't help it. I've smiled more since walking into this shack than I have since leaving home.*

We have a place now, Wolf and I. And we have Sage.

I think we might be okay.

WOLF

Wolf closed the journal and lowered his head. He looked beside him at Camellia, who'd been riveted while he'd read.

"You okay?" she asked. "How do you feel about all this?"

She searched his face. Firelight danced in her eyes. Night insects whirred and, far off, a coyote yipped a lonely song.

"It feels like another layer of knowing. Like some of the missing pieces are snapping into place." He lowered his head, took a deep breath of the air, smelling the river and the hot smoke from their fire. Looking into her eyes too long was doing things to his heartbeat. "I figured if Mom wasn't my mother, Grandma Sage probably wasn't my grandmother." He shrugged. "I mean, I should've figured, us being three difference shades of humanity. But what are the odds? That she just went hiking and found her? That Gram Sage was *expecting* her? That seems like a lot."

"Oh, come on, what if Grandma Sage really *was* in tune, some-how?" Camellia asked. "She said she thought she was near death. I've heard stories like that before. Haven't you?"

"Sure, but..." He lifted his brows. "Do you believe in that kind of thing?"

"Why not? It's more fun to believe than not to," she said. "Don't you?"

"No, I don't think I do."

She blinked at him as if he'd sprouted antlers. "You survived a trip down the Rio Grande as a newborn, and you don't believe in…anything?"

He shrugged. He'd never given that sort of thing much thought until now, but it would make him seem shallow to admit it.

"You should at least be open to the possibility," she said. "You never know."

He rolled his eyes.

"Okay, fine, new topic. You want to know *my* takeaway from tonight's reading?"

He met her eyes again, nodded twice.

"We can probably find that shack, if there's anything left of it."

His jaw dropped and he clamped it again. "I can't believe I didn't think of that."

"I can. You were distracted, filling in the blank parts of your history. I think there are more pieces to be found in this park. I think that shack's the first one, and I think it'll lead us to the next."

He sighed, shaking his head in wonder, then said, "You're kind of brilliant, Camellia Rio."

"I think it's more that *you're* kind of distracted."

"I am, for sure." And not just by the diary, or being so near the spot where he'd been found in the river, though both those things were a constant background hum. No, it was something more immediate, or a mix of things. The quiet, and the underlying rhythmic song of whatever bugs were whirring and chirping in perfect million-part harmony, and the darkness all around them seemed to push them closer. The lure of the fire, snapping nearby, cast orange light and amber shadows across their faces. It was intimate, and the air tasted of woodsmoke. He cleared his throat.

Something shifted between them, there in the quiet. Something changed. He wondered if she felt it, too, looked to see, and got stuck in her eyes.

"It's cold." She said it, he thought, for something to say, but her eyes were still locked with his.

"Should we—?" he began.

"We should get hot cocoa!" She jumped to her feet with the words. Then, looking toward the path added, "Or something else warm. There was a place near where we got the sandwiches. It gets dark so early this time of year. It's only"—she glanced at her phone—"eight twenty-one."

"The Rio Grande Cantina," he said. "That was the name, wasn't it?" It was only a fifteen-minute walk. He'd scared her, he realized. Or something had. Maybe she'd felt things shift between them, too. And this was her reaction.

Not exactly a big green light.

He didn't like making her nervous, and he hadn't meant to reveal his attraction or make her uncomfortable.

"There was a camping gear place near there, too," he said, trying to figure out how to ease her mind. "We could even grab a second tent, if—"

"We might need all our body heat in one, as chilly as it is tonight," she said. "Besides, I trust you." She reached for his hand, and when he took it, tugged him out of his chair. "Besides, there's a room-divider that zips right across the middle of the tent, if you get out of line." She narrowed her eyes at him in mock menace.

She was witty and quick and dang near the prettiest thing Wolf had ever seen.

They started walking together, their hands parting naturally but touching now and then as they headed up the path from their campsite to the narrow, paved lane and then down it toward the village. They walked in silence, while he tried to put words together. He liked to think before he spoke, so his words meant something when he said them. It took until they were entering the small cluster of buildings for him to say, "That means a lot to me, you saying you trust me. I trust you, too,

Camellia, which is weird, because I've been raised to not trust people."

"I know you have," she said. "And I also know you trust me. I mean, you're letting me read your mother's journals. That says a lot." She sent him a crooked smile.

"Don't let that feel like pressure though, as far as the case goes," he said. "I know you're only human."

"Dang, here I was hoping you thought I was supernatural."

You kind of are. Wolf bit his lip to keep that particular thought from leaking through.

CHAPTER EIGHT

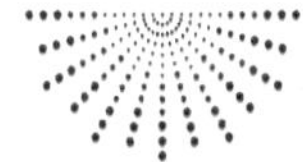

CAMELLIA

The village consisted of a souvenir shop, three places to eat, one bar, a supply store with a post office inside, and a stand that sold charcoal and bundles of firewood, during seasons when fires were permitted. It also contained too many people.

Camellia had suffered some very real PTSD during and after Earl's stalking. She'd been over it until that phone call, but since then, she'd felt it stirring inside her.

Until this place. Here, she'd been feeling safer and safer, tucked away in the wilderness, all alone with a beautiful, gentle man.

But now she was out among people again, and it felt like her security blanket had fallen away. All her old fears were nipping at her heels.

Her phone, in her pocket as always, made a sound, and she said, "A signal. What do you know?"

"That's handy." He pulled out his own phone, glanced at it, then looked sad.

Camellia knew his first instinct had probably been to check for messages from his mom. She gave his arm a squeeze and checked her own messages. "Oh, hey, there's text from Detective Simms. Several texts," she said, scrolling, reading. "She checked into Mary Jo Gallagher's suicide."

"Earl's girlfriend," he said, and she nodded.

"There's no evidence of foul play."

She texted back a thank you but didn't expect a reply. It was after hours.

It was a sad kind of relief to know that Earl's girlfriend had taken her own life, even though she suspected he might've driven her to it. But they were far away from him, Camellia reminded herself. She was safe here.

There was a lot of activity over by the bicycle rental kiosk, and not for the bikes. The booth was lined with maps and flyers. A book on the counter like the one where they'd signed in had one person after another flipping its pages.

"What do you think that's about?" She looked up at Wolf as she asked it and was struck again by how handsome he was. She'd been feeling things back there at the campsite—like her whole body had been infused by the firelight.

But gosh, she'd told him in no uncertain terms she wasn't interested. She'd look like an idiot if she went back on it, wouldn't she?

"We can find out," Wolf said. Then he walked over there. She didn't go with him. There were chills chasing each other up her spine, like eyes on her back. It was so real that she turned to look behind her. Someone was walking away up the path. Someone with a familiar shape and posture and gait. She gasped and whirled right into Wolf's chest.

His hands came to her shoulders. "Hey," he said, and when she looked up, he met her eyes and frowned. "What happened?"

"I think I saw him. Earl, he's—" She turned, pointing, but the road was dark and the only people on it were a group of teenagers in backpacks, heading toward them, not away.

Wolf looked from the road back to her face. "We can call the police. Are you sure it was him?"

She closed her eyes, shook her head. "I didn't see his face. It was too dark, he was too far away, and I could only see the back of him, but his shape, and the way he moved…" She sighed and lowered her head. "I sound like a crazy person."

"If you say it was him, I believe you."

She took a deep breath, replaying the whole thing in her mind. "No, I can't even convince myself, for sure. I'm triggered, I think. It felt so safe and secluded at our site."

He sighed heavily and looked around the place, probably in search of something that would make her feel better. He was thoughtful that way.

"What's the deal at the kiosk?" she asked to change the subject.

"It's just a sign-in book, like the one at every gate. There's a large group on separate sites, trying to find each other."

Camellia frowned and looked that way. "Anyone can just look in the book and find what site you're on. I hadn't thought of that."

"Looks that way. We're not in that book, though."

"We're in one of them."

"Yeah, but we're not in our assigned site. Nobody can find us that way, Camellia."

The way her name sounded on his lips gave her a whole different set of chills. He pronounced both Ls or something and made it sound more beautiful than it had ever sounded to her.

"We can check the books, too," he suggested. "See if he's registered."

"He wouldn't have used his real name."

"They looked at our ID, though. He carry a fake ID around with him, to your knowledge?"

She shook her head, sighed. "I'm just jumpy. It probably wasn't even him."

"We don't have to stay—"

"Yes, we do." She nodded at one of the diners. "They close soon. Let's get churros. Better than cocoa!"

"Sure." They went into a sit-down Mexican restaurant and ordered churros and coffee. Soft Spanish guitar came from speakers mounted along with the cameras in the upper corners of the small dining room. Booths of red Formica with seats upholstered in green lined three walls. A counter stretched across the fourth wall, and tables filled the space in between. Camellia picked a small booth in the back corner where she could see everyone in the place.

It wasn't logical to think she'd seen Earl. There was no evidence to support her having seen him.

There was that black Chevy Blazer on the highway.

But that was two hundred miles from here.

Okay, one scant piece of evidence, and a weak one—a car he might not even have anymore, for all she knew. It was still registered to him, though.

But no, she'd glimpsed a fellow camper with a similar build from a distance in the dark. It wasn't enough to worry about, much less enough to distract her from Wolf's case.

Their order came, and they dug in. There wasn't a lot of conversation after that.

When they finished and left the establishment, Wolf veered into the souvenir shop next door, clasping her elbow and steering her right in there with him. He walked through the place with purpose, on a mission, snatching a pair of baseball caps with the park logo on them. He plopped one onto her head, and one onto his own. Then he went to the spinning rack of sunglasses and gave it a slow turn before plucking a big round purple pair that would've made Elton John blush and slid them right onto her face.

"What are you doing?" she asked around her laughter.

He put on a pair of Aviators and blinked at the mirror, and she laughed even more. He was soothing her nerves with his antics, if nothing else. And she appreciated the distraction. He leaned in, putting his hand to one side of his mouth, and stage whispered, "I'm getting our disguises together. Do you think they have any of those wax lips?"

"I thought those had gone extinct."

"Covid masks?" he asked, nodding toward a rack of them in floral and leafy patterns.

She removed the huge glasses and said, "If we're wearing these at night, we need lighter lenses. Ohhh, like these." She picked up a pair with bright yellow lenses and a dangling "Night vision that darkens by day" tag. They were aviator-shaped and too big for her face, but she liked them.

"Done."

She took off the baseball cap and put on a fishing hat instead. "More brim means less visibility."

"I'll keep this one," he said. "Flatters my jawline. Besides." He turned around and pulled his long dark hair right through the opening in the back of the hat. "Built-in hair band."

"Anything else?" she asked.

"Shop's closing, folks," called a man with a bushy gray beard who was running the place from behind his counter.

"Guess not," Camellia said, and they wore their purchases to the counter, peeling off the tags as they went.

"Hey, I have an idea," Wolf said while the cashier rang up the tags they'd removed from their getup. "Let's not take the road back. Let's walk along the river's edge. There's a trail. I saw a sign."

"You have flashlights?" the clerk asked, pointing to a display on the wall, no longer in such a hurry to close.

"No, but we'll take two of those big ones that look like they could double as weapons in a pinch," Camellia said. "Are a dozen D batteries included?"

The clerk's frown was the same as if she'd asked whether he'd ever been abducted by aliens.

"And batteries," she added quickly.

Wolf laughed softly beside her. She looked over at him, but he was well-hidden behind his sunglasses and baseball cap.

The trail was nice, lined in red sand, without pits or holes. It meandered with the river, only a few yards from its edge, but sometimes veering farther from the banks to go around trees or rock formations. The ground sloped downward toward the water, all earth and stone and scraggly grasses. They kept their flashlight beams aimed toward the water, and she knew he was looking for spots where his mother might've found him. She couldn't stop envisioning him, a little baby lying in the water, cold and alone and in so much danger, after surviving who knew what hell?

Just as she thought it, her flashlight beam picked out a small brown face with water lapping over it.

She gulped back a shriek and ran down the slope and right into the cold water, through floating debris. She fell, submerged entirely, then got upright again and kept sloshing toward the face beneath the waves. Wolf came splashing up behind her as she reached for the drowned baby and picked it up out of the water.

Wolf waded closer and closed his hands around her shoulders as she touched the mildewed face and nearly went limp. "It's a doll. Oh my God, it's a doll. It's just a doll." She let the thing fall from her hands, turned, and wrapped her arms around Wolf. "I'm so sorry that happened to you, Wolf. I'm so damn sorry." She didn't mean to cry, but she did, and she felt stupid for crying because this wasn't about her. The thought of him lying there with the water lapping over his beautiful face just gutted her every time it came into her mind. She hugged her arms tighter around his waist, her face pressed to his chest and soaking wet shirt.

He put his hands into her hair and tipped her head up. He had tears in his eyes, too. She lifted her chin ever so slightly, and he lowered his head. When their lips touched, they were salty and wet. They stood there kissing, all wrapped in each other, for a long time.

When they parted, his forehead rested against hers. He didn't say anything, and she didn't either. They stepped apart, arms still anchored though, as they waded up out of the shallow water. She moved her light around as they did. Wolf's flashlight was on the path. She could see its beam where he'd dropped it.

"Look at all this stuff," she said as the light's beam picked out empty bottles, cans, cups, and litter of all sorts forming a foot-wide border between river and shore, but only in this one little spot.

"Garbage," Wolf said. He steadied her as she got up onto dry land before joining her there. "The current dumps it here natu-rally." He looked into her eyes.

"This might be where you wound up, Wolf, but it doesn't make you garbage. Your mother found treasure here. *You* were a treasure to her," she said, nearly quoting the words in his moth-er's journal.

He looked at the water for a long moment before he started walking again. "Her first campsite would have been near here, then," he said. "According to the diaries. We must've got pretty close to it when we chose ours."

"Wait, look!" She pointed to a finger of ground that jutted into the river, forcing it to bend around, a few yards behind them. "That's where the people were today. Remember? The ones we saw from the cliff? We walked right by it and didn't realize. Come on."

She grabbed his hand, and they hurried to the spot. Camellia shone the flashlight around, stopping immediately on a small pile of stones. "That's not natural. Somebody put that there." And as she ran closer, Wolf stayed behind.

She knelt near the stones. Wolf whispered, "Camellia, don't."

"There's something underneath, I can see it."

"Leave it alone. It might be sacred or something. And it's none of our business."

His voice shook, though, and when she looked up at him staring at that cairn, she thought she saw fear in his eyes.

WILLOW BRAND, BIG BEND NATIONAL PARK

They'd beached their boats at the end of the river ride. Then the canoes were loaded onto a trailer, and Willow and her cousins were all herded into a van and driven back to where they'd started.

The entire time Willow had stayed quiet, and if her cousins seemed uneasy, it was probably because they weren't used to seeing her so shaken.

Then again, they'd just held a memorial for the dead brother she never knew she had, so she supposed some grieving was to be expected.

Back at the tiny square building that housed the offices of Big Bend River Rides, they stood around their rented van talking while Drew went inside to settle up.

Ethan said, "I felt good about this. Willow, I'm glad you had the idea."

"Yeah, this was great, Will," Maria added. "Your brother would be—"

"I'm not goin' home." Willow blurted it just as Drew rejoined them. She'd been ready to blurt it for a while now. "I'm staying close."

"But Willow, why?" Maria-Michelle asked.

"Because…" Willow looked around at all her cousins, then closed her eyes, gathering courage before she spoke again. They were all going to think she'd lost it. "I think he might still be alive."

Ethan said, "Oh, come on, Will."

At the same time, Maria said, "*Seriously?*"

"I think there's a chance. I'm going back there to that inlet with the refuse, near where we did the ceremony, and I'm gonna find proof, one way or the other."

"Honey, be logical. What proof could there be after twenty-eight years?" Maria asked.

"Sometimes you have to put logic aside," said Orrin.

Orrin was the quiet, brooding cousin. Bubbly blond Drew's equally blond but far less bubbly brother. "I'll stay with you, Willow," he said.

"Me, too," Maria said quickly. "But um, we didn't bring any camping gear, did we?"

"I texted a friend with a hunting cabin right up against the park's boundary," Willow replied, turning her phone face-out to show a shot of the little log cabin her friend had texted her. "It's even on the side of the park we want. How many are coming with?"

She looked around at each face. She saw worry in their eyes, yeah, and doubt too, but mostly resignation. If one Brand was staying, they were all staying. She hadn't even needed to ask.

WOLF

Wolf laid on his back, the sleeping bag tight around him. He was cold. His tent mate, however, was shivering. He could feel her shaking right beside him.

"You're freezing, Camellia."

They had returned to the tent, soaked and frozen by the time they got there, then quickly put on dry clothes and zipped themselves into their respective sleeping bags. "I h-have a p-portable h-heater somewhere."

"We didn't expect it to b-be this cold." He got out of his sleeping bag, found the small heater, and turned it on. Nothing happened. "I thought we got batteries."

"Shoot, I f-forgot. That one's rechargeable," she said.

And uncharged, so he dove back into his sleeping bag.

They had not discussed their passionate, river-soaked kissing. He didn't know what to say about it, and he hoped she still felt safe with him after all that, because he was about to put it to the test.

He sat up fast, unzipped his bag, and said, "Come on, we have no choice but to double up. I promise I won't turn into a Neanderthal in my sleep. You can trust me."

"It's n-not that," she said, but she sat up, unzipped, and offered him the end of her sleeping bag.

There was nothing very sexy about it. They'd both donned sweatpants and shirts to try to get warm. He quickly zipped his bag to hers, duck-walking all the way around the shivering woman to create a large double sleeping bag. He left his side open just enough to slide in. His legs brushed hers as he did, but there was no helping it.

He got settled more or less, lying on his back, stiff and still cold. "It's okay. I don't blame you for not liking this. We haven't known each other that long."

"It's not that." She sat up and pulled a green hairpin from her hair, and the waves fell around her like a butterscotch waterfall.

Wolf's breath escaped all at once and every thought in his head ground to a halt. He'd been wanting to see her hair down ever since he'd met her, which yes, was weird, but he chalked it up to curiosity and an appreciation of natural beauty. Nothing personal about it. Except now he knew better, and especially since that kiss. Whatever was brewing between them was *very* personal.

Her hair was longer than he'd guessed, and he'd guessed long. It fell, all waves and gentle curls, past her shoulders and halfway down her upper arms. And as she shook it gently, freeing it from its daytime clusters, she said, "Shoot, after that kiss earlier, I'm not sure I trust *me*."

He turned his head toward her sharply, not sure he'd heard her right.

"We'll just have to do the best we can, though."

Well, what the hell did *that* mean?

She rolled toward him and snuggled right up close, resting her head on his chest, draping her arm across his waist, with her legs pressed to his for warmth. He closed his left arm loosely around her shoulders, because with her lying in its crook, there wasn't much else he could do with it. He prayed he wouldn't wind up poking her with an erection before dawn and laid perfectly still.

After a few moments, she stopped shivering and released a long, heavy sigh, with a delicate snore at the end. He laughed in spite of himself, but kept it silent and hoped the movement of his chest wouldn't wake her.

It didn't. She was sound asleep, and he finally relaxed. As soon as he did, her warmth suffused him, and he found he wasn't cold anymore. She snuggled a little closer, and he just let it happen. All that glorious hair was on his chest and tickling his chin, and he resented the shirt he'd put on.

Camellia in his arms felt better than anything had in a long time—not counting the kisses, which had felt like pure fire.

By the time morning came, they were tangled around each other like a pair of spider monkeys, but warm, cozy, comfy. She had a leg over one of his and under the other, and he was hugging her like she'd float away if he let go. Dang, he didn't want to disengage his limbs from hers and get out of their nest to face the chilly morning, but he figured it best he do so before she woke up.

Then she did, and it was too late. She lifted her head off his chest, looked up into his face from within that mass of glorious hair, and beamed him a smile. "Guess we stayed warm enough."

"Downright snug," he replied, but he couldn't roll over and get out, because she was still mostly on top of him—and his blood was heading to places he didn't need it to be heading just then.

"Okay, easing out now," he said. He lifted her shoulders off his chest so he could slide out from under her.

She made a sad noise, but she let him go. He rolled out, then turned around, looking for the clothes he'd left close by for quick dressing.

"Oh, wait!" Camellia vanished under the covers entirely. When she came out, she handed him his clothes, which had been a neatly folded stack and now were a wadded-up bundle. "I grabbed them when I got up to pee," she said. "Figured they'd be nice and warm to put on."

He must have slept through that. It worried him that he didn't remember.

He took the bundle from her, and then she vanished beneath the sleeping bags again. "Go ahead and dress," she called, her voice muffled. "I won't peek."

He got dressed, and she was right, the clothes were much warmer than they'd have been had they sat out in the tent all night. When she popped out from the sleeping bags again, she came all the way out, wearing fresh jeans and a T-shirt with an unzipped hoodie over it. She sat on top of their sleeping bags and pulled on a pair of socks, then her hiking boots. And then she said, "So? Was that as hard for you as it was for me?"

He pretended not to understand what she was getting at,

because he wasn't sure he did. He knew what he *thought* she meant, but that had to be wrong.

"What do you mean?" he asked, pulling on a jacket and moving the grocery bags off to one side of the tent. "Is the coffee in here?" He knelt and dug until he found a pound of ground roast.

She hadn't replied, so he glanced her way to find her sitting there looking at him oddly. She wore a slight frown and had her head tilted to one side. But she didn't say anything.

"You think there are still coals in the fire?" he asked.

"Huh," she said. "Okay."

"Okay what?"

She shrugged. "The fire'll be dead, but the little two-burner cooktop is out there, and we hooked up a fresh tank of propane, so go for it."

"Cool." He grabbed the coffeepot, which was a blue metal percolator with white spots. His mom's kitchen had a shiny silver percolator that plugged in, and he figured this couldn't be much different. He headed outside, uneasy. Clearly Camellia had wanted to talk about...what? Their kissing yesterday and then sleeping together without letting anything happen, he guessed. And if she thought for one second that had been harder for her than it had been for him, then she didn't know much about the male anatomy.

He poured water from a jug into the coffeepot, guessed at the amount of grounds to put into the basket, popped on the lid, and set it on the burner. Easy. He figured he'd let it brew until the color looked right in the clear glass bubble on top. The one at home timed itself.

Inside the tent, Camellia was moving around doing whatever women did. He reviewed her question. Had it been hard? Yeah, *it* had been hard all night, and he'd barely slept. And he liked her more every minute he spent with her, and he'd told her he had no interest in getting involved, and that was the only reason she'd trusted him.

She trusted him.

And she had a stalker ex that made trusting difficult. He was *not* going to betray that.

She'd only agreed to come with him because he'd assured her sex was the last thing on his mind. If she woke up with a log poking her in the thigh, he figured she'd hightail it home and leave him on his own.

And he just wasn't ready to say goodbye to her.

So, he did the only thing he could think of that was guaranteed not to send her into retreat. He made coffee, sat in his stubby camp chair to watch it brew, and kept his thoughts to himself.

Camellia emerged from the tent just as the percolator got to bubbling a light caramel color. She'd zipped up her jacket and pulled up its hood. "Five more minutes," she said with a nod at the coffeepot. "Here."

She handed him a jumbo-sized granola bar and an orange.

"Breakfast of champions," he said. "Thanks."

"Hm." She sat in her chair and began peeling her fruit.

He opened his granola bar and figured he didn't have to talk and risk screwing this up as long as he was eating, so he took his time and chewed slowly.

She said, "There were clues in that passage from your mom's journal. The day she found Sage's shack. I went back through it and made some notes."

Her voice was a little lower than usual, he thought, and the cadence of her words didn't have their usual lilt or underlying smile. "When did you have time to do that?"

"I stayed up a while. When I got up to pee."

"How did I not—?" And suddenly his blood went cold. "Did I do something out of line? I swear, if I did, I wasn't awake. It wasn't on purpose."

She was just looking at him, expressionless, unblinking.

"Hell," he said. "Camellia, I'm—"

"You didn't lay a finger on me, Wolf. Relax. Your honor is intact." Then she hitched her chin and said, "Coffee's done."

"I got it." He turned off the burner and reached for the two tin cups that matched the pot.

"Might as well fill the travel mugs," Camellia said. "We can get an early start."

Yeah, she was pissed. And he had no idea why. He filled their travel mugs, put on the caps, and handed hers over. "You're good at this detective stuff," he said. "I didn't notice any clues in the journal."

She didn't say anything, just tilted her head to acknowledge she'd heard him and set off walking.

CHAPTER NINE

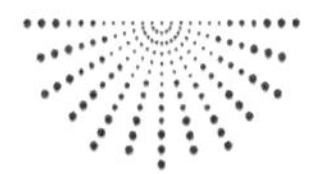

CAMELLIA

*C*amellia took the lead, and she knew her pace was too fast to sustain, but she was walking off some frustration. A couple of times lately, she'd felt something, seen something in Wolf's eyes when they met hers, and then that kiss…

And yet last night, he'd acted like a fourth-grader who thought girls had cooties. He'd been stiff and guarded. Even when she'd snuggled up to let him know it was okay.

Jerk.

Fine. She didn't need his validation.

She hadn't needed his rejection either, though.

Whatever.

"'We were walking right into the sun, we left so early,'" Wolf said, reading from the journal they'd brought along. "'We headed way up into the highest, rockiest places we could see. We went that way often, but this time we went farther from the river, deeper into the wilds. I don't know if we were within the park's boundaries or not.'"

He looked out into the distance ahead of them.

It infuriated Camellia that he was pretending not to know anything was wrong. On the other hand, the only thing wrong was that he hadn't responded to her signals last night.

She was being ridiculous. He couldn't help it if he didn't want to… That kiss in the river had been pure emotion, what with the doll in the water and his history and all. It might not have meant anything.

Although he'd sure seemed attracted to her when they'd been all wrapped in each other's arms, surrounded by the cold rushing river, their only warmth the places where they were pressed together.

She heaved a big, deep sigh and told herself to let it go. Wanting someone who didn't want you back was how you wound up like Earl, obsessed and out of control. Besides, she *had* told him she intended to die single.

They hiked away from their campsite, heading whatever direction went uphill, until they had a beautiful view. Rock formations and scrub brush spread out around them over brown, stony ground with stunted trees clinging in unlikely places. The sky was blue without a cloud in sight, and she was glad of her hat and sunglasses, which darkened, as advertised, in the bright light.

"There," Wolf said, pointing. "Those are the highest rocks I can see."

"I agree. Let's head that way." She took off her backpack, though, and then shucked her hoodie, rolled it up, and tucked it inside where there were several water bottles to refill the canteens they each carried, a paper map, her phone, and her lunch. "It's already warm."

He looked at her curiously, noticing her friendly tone, no doubt. He should. She was trying to take his rejection with grace.

"Didn't take long, did it?" He took off his jacket as well. And she noticed how his T-shirt clung to his chest and remembered how hard it had felt under her hands when they'd kissed. He had some muscles going on under there all right.

She shook her head, disgusted with herself, then stopped all at once, grabbed Wolf's arm, and put a finger to her lips. He went still, too, frowning at her. There were two more sounds, footsteps she thought, somewhere behind them.

He heard them, too. She saw him react. And then the sounds stopped, and it was quiet again. There was no one in sight behind them. She took a deep breath.

"Probably an animal," Wolf said. "Coyote, maybe, or a deer."

She nodded and told her heart to slow down. "Probably," she said.

But she listened, and she watched their backs as they hiked on. She never saw anyone or heard any footsteps again. So why was there a chill dancing up and down her nape every little while?

She'd deliberately lowered her bristles and tried to recapture the easy energy that had existed between her and Wolf up until now. It had been good, maybe the beginning of a solid friendship even, and she didn't want to ruin it.

Soon they were hiking through the high, rocky places. They picked a flat-topped boulder with a view for miles and sat down to take a rest and get their bearings. Wolf dropped everything he was carrying, took out the map, and spread it open atop the boulder.

Camellia picked up his canteen, nudged his arm with it till he took it and drank. Then he pointed to the spot that matched their location. "I think we're about here." She was chugging from her own canteen but nodded as Wolf went on. "Ma wrote that they could see the river, so far away it was no wider than her forefinger."

She finished her drink, wiped her lips with the back of her hand, and screwed its lid back on. Then she got out a package of trail mix, ate a handful, and offered the bag to Wolf.

He took some, too, looking at the horizon and then at the map as he ate. Then he said, "The river's that way from here," and pointed directly toward a row of towering formations.

She said, "Those rocks might be the only thing blocking our view of it. Let's hike out past them next." She drank some more water, ate some more trail mix. He did the same, and then they sealed everything up and returned it to the backpack. "You all rested up?"

"In that forty-five second break we just took, you mean?" He said it with a teasing tone.

That was better. Maybe their friendship was still okay. "It was at least three minutes. Why? Can't you keep up with me?" She sprang to her feet, heading in the direction of the rock formations at a clip that challenged him to catch her.

He did, and they picked their way around the boulders. There was no trail, and they were up high, but as soon as they cleared the formations, the river glinted silver-blue in the distance. Camellia ran up onto a stony rise and held up her forefinger to measure. Then she turned and said, "A little further, I think." And then the ground fell from under her feet and she dropped.

WOLF

"Camellia!"

Wolf watched her vanish and scrambled up onto the small rise as Camellia's body pounded down a steep, rocky slope. He slipped and slid down after her, losing his footing a couple of times along the way before he finally came to rest beside her. She'd landed on her back, but her hair had come loose and covered her face.

He put his hands on her shoulders, leaning over her, pushing the hair away, and thinking again how soft it was against his fingers. "Be okay," he said, and it came out all choked and hoarse.

He got past the tangle of honey-gold to see a pair of dark blue eyes blinking at him.

"Are you hurt?"

"I'm…checking," she said, moving very slowly.

He closed his arms around her, hugging her upper body against his chest. He did it without thinking, and just held her there against him, feeling her heart beat on the side of his chest where his didn't, and a yin-yang symbol flashed white-hot in his brain.

When he released her, her face was near his, and he looked at her mouth and almost kissed her.

She looked right back at him, and he was pretty sure she'd have let him.

Then he looked away and broke the spell, releasing her, as she was sitting upright on her own.

She looked at her arms, moved her legs, and nodded. "I don't think anything's broken. And I don't see any blood. But yeah. It hurts."

He got to his feet and reached a hand down for her. She clasped it and let him pull her upright. As she stood there looking up at him, the wind came and lifted her hair like a golden cloud around her. He got lost in it for a second, and she leaned a little closer. Then the wind died and her hair settled around her shoulders, revealing the shape of a broken-down structure in the distance behind her.

CAMELLIA

His hands were still on her shoulders and his eyes shifted to hers.

"What?" she asked. *Is he going to kiss me or not?*

He shifted his gaze to what stood in the distance behind her, then turned her around until she saw the shack, or what was left of it.

"Holy— Do you think that's it?" she whispered.

"Has to be," he whispered back.

It felt to Camellia like if they spoke too loud, the illusion might shatter.

They made their way to the shack, which was farther than it looked, but eventually, they stood outside the broken-down remnants of the small building. It'd once had four walls and a roof. It currently had two walls leaning inward against each other, and the roof appeared to have melted into the ground where the other two walls had collapsed. An entire eco-system of vegetation covered most of the exposed wood, and some kind of moss or algae clung to the black roof.

Wolf stood there staring at it, and his eyes were filled with shadows of the past.

"Do you remember anything, Wolf?"

"I played here," he said. "There was a shed there and shaded gardens out beyond those rocks."

He nodded, spread his fingers near the side of his head. "Memories fade in and out like ghosts. Like they've been in there all along."

"Tell me," she said. "It might help you to not forget them again."

He nodded, looking around. "There was a small shed—we called it a barn—over there." He walked to the spot and knelt, brushed dirt away with his hands.

"We should've brought shovels," Camellia said. "I didn't know we'd be doing archeology."

"I was going to become an archaeologist from third to seventh grade," he told her.

"Yeah?" She was smiling up at him. His shock seemed to be wearing off. He was getting excited now. "And what happened?"

"I discovered girls."

She laughed, then clasped his shoulder once, before kneeling beside him to begin brushing dirt away. Eventually, they uncovered a few rotted boards, enough to confirm his memory.

He got up slowly, turned, and said, "There was a spring in those rocks." Then he jogged toward the cluster of boulders anchored deep in the earth, and the spring was there, bubbling up into a tiny stone basin within. "We kept food cold in here. There was a deeper well with a hand pump closer to the house for drinking water."

"And there's the view of the river she mentioned," Camellia said, holding up a finger to measure. "But where's the Wile E. Coyote formation?"

They both looked around for a long moment. Wolf spotted it first and nudged her shoulder with his. "There."

The oblong boulder that Cilla had described as being balanced on top of a stone column as if waiting for the Road Runner's coyote to come by, lay instead beside it, one end still propped up against its former base.

"Guess the coyote was here," Wolf said.

Camellia turned. "You think there's anything left inside the shack?"

A strange male voice said, "Nope," and she dang near jumped out of her skin.

WOLF

Wolf put an arm around Camellia, pulling her behind him as he stepped in front, facing the newcomer, an old man in a park ranger uniform that hung loose on his skinny frame. His tan shorts came to mid-thigh, and his campaign hat caused a shadow to cut across his face, but not enough to hide the wrinkles.

"Officer," Wolf said, dipping his head.

"Ranger," he corrected. "Ranger Dan." And he tapped his badge.

"Can we help you, Ranger Dan?"

The old man gazed at Wolf, then narrowed his eyes and took a step closer. "Are you him, then? Wolf Travail?"

The shock that rippled through him was beyond anything Wolf had felt before. "How do you—?"

"You *know* him?" Camellia asked, pushing out from behind him.

"Knew his grandma," the ranger said, and his lips pulled into a smile as he said it, one he quickly hid by running his hand across his whiskered mouth. "I expect you have questions, if you're him."

"I'm him," Wolf said. And he fought to calm down. His heart was going a hundred miles an hour. This might be nothing. And why was he excited anyway, when he didn't even really *want* to find his family? He just wanted to extend his time around Camellia in hopes he'd be in close proximity if she changed her mind about dying single.

He shook all that off and refocused on the old man. "Care to sit? We have water."

He nodded and took a seat on a red-brown boulder that protruded from the ground amid several others. Wolf sat on a rock to his left. Camellia offered her canteen, but Ranger Dan took his own from his belt. As he tipped his head back to drink, he swept off his hat with his other hand, moved the canteen up, and poured water over his head, revealing sparse gray hairs combed from one side to the other, which he ruffled before replacing the hat.

"Ahh. Good water here. Sweet," he said. "I don't have all that much to tell you. I discovered the women squatting out here, and"—he nodded at Wolf—"the child. I was trailing a wolf that'd been menacing campers. Never did find it. It led me to the three of you, though."

"Holy shit," Camellia said, rubbed her arms, and shot wide eyes to Wolf.

He gave her a skeptical smirk and subtle head shake in the direction of no. He only believed in what he could see.

"Your mother went by Cilla back then," Ranger Dan said. "She wouldn't so much as talk to me. Took you and left in a huff whenever I came by to see Sage." The old man's weathered face sported a day's growth of mostly white whiskers.

"You didn't turn us in?" Wolf asked. He didn't much care about finding his family, but for some reason his stomach was churning and his heart was beating too hard.

The ranger shrugged. "You weren't hurting anybody. Sage and I, we had a connection for a time. I used to bring up supplies whenever I could. Then one day, you all were just gone. You were about four years old, I believe, and I know Sage had been worried about getting you into school. My guess was they took you some-place where that could happen."

Wolf nodded. "I remember starting kindergarten. We lived… in a town." He strained his mind for more details, but none came.

"Those women took everything they owned with 'em when they left, I'll tell you what," the old man said. "It if wasn't nailed down, it was no longer there. Lord knows I searched for any clue where you'd all gone, but…" He lowered his head, shaking it slowly. Then raising it again, he met Wolf's eyes. "I hope that's of some help to you."

"It's more than we knew before," he said. "Thank you."

"I seen you coming up here, had a feeling."

"Oh, that was you?" Camellia asked.

"What now, Miss?"

She came up beside Wolf and spoke to the ranger. "I kept feeling like someone was on the trail behind us as we hiked up. It must've been you, right?"

He raised his white eyebrows and shook his head. "I was farther up, that a'way." He pointed in the opposite direction from which they'd come. "I could see you coming up the trail from there."

"Oh," she said.

"What were you doing way up there?" Wolf asked. "It seems a long hike for—"

"For an old man, yeah, I know. That wolf showed up again, and I tracked him up there. Odd, I ain't seen him once in *all this time*." He added a mystical lilt to his voice on the final three words.

Wolf lowered his head to hide an amused smile and ignored the chill that went up his spine. The old ranger said, "I'm expected back. They get nervous if I'm late and pretend it's not due to my age. You all enjoy yourselves now. Watch the drop-offs if you stay past dark, all righty?"

"Sure," Wolf said. "And thank you."

The ranger started to turn away, then Wolf said, "Hey, you uh—you're not gonna shoot that wolf, are you?"

Ranger Dan turned back and patted the ammo belt around his waist. It was filled with darts, not bullets. "Only a tranq so we can relocate him, and only if I have to. This is his home. We're the invaders, so unless he's literally eating campers, I'm not apt to do him any harm."

He was about to turn away, but once more hesitated. "Almost forgot—*had* forgot, for years. I've been going through my daily logs, reviewing my days as a ranger before I retire in a few weeks. I have some stories to tell, I'll tell you what!"

"Maybe you should write a memoir," Camellia said.

He lit right up. "That's what I'm thinking, young lady. Anyway, I found a note I'd forgot all about, and I never made the connection till now. It might not mean much, but a sheriff come around here looking for a lost baby. Must've been a full six months before I stumbled upon you and Cilla and Sage, and I'd forgot all about him by then."

The words hit Wolf like a mallet between the eyes. "Did you write down *what* sheriff? His name, or where he was from?"

Ranger Dan shook his head slowly. "Big man, he was. Honest face. From upriver, I believe." Then he scraped his face with his hand again, like he was feeling around in his whiskers for answers. "That's everything, son. Believe me, once I found that note, I hunted through everything I had. It's only now I've been putting it together myself."

Then he blinked slowly, looking into Wolf's eyes. "She's passed, hasn't she? Sage?"

"They both have," Wolf said. "Grandma Sage when I was sixteen, and my mother two weeks ago."

The old man looked at the ground. "No, that's too young," he said, shaking his head. "I'm real sorry to hear that. Special women, Sage and Cilla both. But closed off, you know? They lived behind a wall."

"Yeah, I know. I lived there with 'em." When he said it, he looked at Camellia and her eyes held on until he could break his free.

"If you find anything else, or remember anything, will you let me know?" Wolf asked.

"Sure. What site you all on?"

"It's number three one nine," Camellia offered. Wolf had not even noticed a number on their site.

The ranger waved, then headed off in a downhill direction.

Wolf watched him move out of sight, then sank back onto his boulder. He didn't plan to, his legs just decided not to hold him upright anymore.

Camellia came over and sank right down beside him. "You see? They *did* look for you," she said.

"Yeah. I just wish we'd found a clue up here."

"That's a *huge* clue, Wolf. Somebody was looking for you. That means you have a birth family."

"I have one large sheriff," he said. "That's hardly a family."

"It's a start."

She squeezed his shoulder, and it felt like comfort. "Let's stay here a while," he said.

She said, "There's shade over there in the shack, beside those leaning walls. And we still have snacks, and a chunk of that journal left to read. You bring it?"

He slid off his boulder. "'Course I brought it." They were on the second volume, yellow cloth-covered cardboard with embroidered daisies. It had a tiny, useless lock, and its key was threaded through the clasp by a thin yellow ribbon.

The journal of a fifteen-year-old mother-by-choice, or maybe by fate. The opening date would have made Wolf four years old.

CILLA

September 17

Today we moved into our first real home. It's an apartment on the ground floor of a farmhouse that was divided into two. And the folks upstairs don't care if we use the dirt patch backyard to keep growing our herbs. We doubled our herb production this year and put almost every penny away till we had enough for this place. I stole stuff from the campground that could be sold quick and easy, too.

I came up with the idea to make herbal sachet bags like those I'd seen my mom use, stuffed with rice or beans and a pinch or two of herbs. Just enough to smell good. Mom would heat them in the microwave and lay them over her eyes when she had one of her headaches. So we made a pile of those and increased the revenue from our herbs by ten times more than selling them by the gram.

I feel like we could've stayed where we were forever and got by. But Wolf is four years old now, calling us Mamma and Grandma. We both know we have to go back to the civilized world. He'll need to go to school. How will he make his way in this world if he doesn't even get a basic education?

He has a birth certificate with his name on it. Wolf Travail. Sage knew a midwife, and she also knew what form to forge her name on, attesting to our boy's home birth. We gave him the date I found him on the riverbank, September 15th, as his birthday.

For the past two months, I've been riding my bike to the bus station in town, and taking a bus to a different location to scope it out for our new home. Sage told me what to look for. Good schools, people who mind their own business, not too poor but not too wealthy, and on the low side of middle class, with plenty of employment nearby. A tourist town would be a plus, Sage said, but we didn't want to live in one, just near one.

And so today, we moved into our new place on the ground floor of a friendly old farmhouse.

We sold our entire stock of dried herbs, herbal teas, eye-pillows, and stolen camping gear, everything we had left all at once, and used the proceeds to have our own fake identification custom-made for us in a border town, where you could get just about anything for a price. It was more expensive to choose our own names, rather than take on the iden-tity of someone who'd died young, but Sage wanted no part in stealing a dead woman's name. So she became Sage Travail, and I remained Cilla.

Our backstory was that Sage's son, Johnny, had been my husband, but he died of pneumonia, as had Sage's own husband only two years earlier. He'd been of Native descent, hence Wolf's appearance.

Sage came up with that tale so easily and with so much emotion in her eyes that I think it was based on the truth. She must've lost a son and a husband. That explains the photo of a young Black man holding a small baby in his arms. Sage keeps it tucked inside the pages of an elaborately illustrated copy of Alice in Wonderland *with an embossed hard cover.*

She doesn't know I've seen the photo. I saw it when we were packing up to move and I flipped through the enticing book's pages. I figure if Sage wants to talk about the young man in the picture, she will.

Now though, I think I know.

WILLOW

Willow stood watching the sunset, near their dwindling campfire.

She'd slipped away from everyone for a moment to reflect. It was chilly down here at night. Cooler than home, though further south, which she found odd. But home was nigh on desert and pancake flat. This place was far different. Texas wasn't one land, but many. A geologic crazy quilt.

"Am I ever going to find you, my brother?" she whispered. And a tear slid from her eyes, trailing slowly down her cheek.

She heard the creak of a door opening, then closing again, and turned to see Drew, tiptoeing her way over the hardpack toward her. "You okay?"

"I'm okay." She wasn't.

"No, you're not." Drew ran her thumb over Willow's cheek, absorbing the tear. "I'm on your side here, cuz."

Willow covered Drew's smaller hand with hers. "You don't think I'm on a wild goose chase?"

"Maybe we are," Drew said, and Willow appreciated her making it about all of them. "But I don't want to go home until I'm sure we've found everything there is to find here. And I'm not there yet."

"Good. That's good," Willow said.

"I think we might want to send Ethan back to the ranch

though. He's uneasy being four hours from Lily this late in her pregnancy. And for good reason, you know?"

"Pregnancy's a dangerous time for a woman, I know." She sighed. "So were you the one elected to come out and talk sense to me?"

"There was no family meeting or anything. I'm just telling you what I'm picking up on. I assume you've talked to Jeremiah about staying the night out here?"

Willow nodded. "He doesn't disagree with me. Says he's got my back, right or wrong, and he doesn't much care which it is. Also, and this is a quote, 'The kid and the dog and I are fine. Do whatever you need to do.'"

Drew gave an overly dramatic sigh. "I want that someday."

"You'll have it someday. Anything ever happen with that young sketch artist you were dating?"

"Mmm, he's in and out of town. Travels for work and visits his fam. It's not…solid, I guess is the word. It's just fun. Casual."

"You'll find the one, Drew. Be patient."

"Fortunately, finding a man is not my top goal in life. I'm more interested in getting my PI biz off the ground, and…" She trailed off, took a breath, bit her lip.

"What?" Willow asked.

Drew said, "This is between us, but Orrin doesn't want to."

"What? But you two were planning to be partners, go into business together. Brand & Brand Investigations."

"I *know*."

"Well, what does he want to do instead?" Willow asked.

"Says he doesn't know, but it isn't this."

"Aw, poor Drew." Willow slid an arm around her younger cousin's shoulders. "What are you fixin' to do about it?"

Drew shrugged. "He only just told me on this trip, so…I'm still processing."

Willow gave her shoulders a squeeze, then let go and rubbed her own arms against the chill that came in as soon as the sun went down. "You think we'll ever know for sure what happened to my brother?"

"I think some*body*, some*where*, knows some*thing*. I don't know if we'll find that person or not, but I think they exist, and as long as the truth is out there, we have a chance of finding it. We haven't failed. This might take some time, though." She sighed heavily. "Publicity would help. One of those missing persons TV shows, you know? But your mom—"

"She couldn't take it. Dad would be furious. He's so protective of her."

"It's sweet, isn't it?"

"He loves her," Willow said. "I don't blame him. I think we'd better exhaust every other possibility before we talk about publicity."

"I concur," Drew said. "We should canvas the nearby towns, and maybe the employees at the campground. See if there are any local legends about a river-baby, hmm?"

"River-baby," Willow repeated, rolling her eyes. "I love you, Drew."

CHAPTER TEN

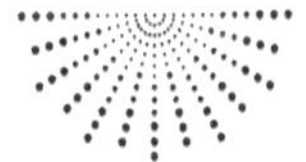

CAMELLIA

Camellia kept her apprehension to herself, because this was such an important moment for Wolf. They'd lingered all day in the place where he'd spent the first four years of his life, talking to someone who'd witnessed a small part of it, recovering memories long since tucked away, reading snippets of his past in his mother's diaries.

Now the sun was setting, and Camellia's feeling of dread had still not faded.

As they started hiking back, she held it inside. She'd started to relax when they'd left Hobbsville to drive from the top of Texas to the bottom—right up until she'd seen that black Blazer on the highway, so much like Earl's. And then that shape in the darkness last night, walking up the trail. And the footsteps she was sure she'd heard behind them today.

She was nervous and half-convinced it was just the old PTSD, reactivated by Earl's phone call. And so there was no point distracting herself, or Wolf, from his quest for his family. Especially not when it was going so well.

"Are you worried that we don't have another clue yet?" he asked as they walked.

"A sheriff from upriver? You think that's not a clue? There are only so many counties between here and there."

"He might not even be alive by now."

"But he might." She walked a little closer beside him, then reminded herself he didn't feel the way she did and allowed a bit more space between them. "It gives us a next step. That's all investigative work is, you know, just finding the next step, and then the next. You never see the whole path. It's like driving at night. You see only as far as your headlights reach."

"That sounds like a wise outlook."

"That's a direct quote from my instructor in that accelerated licensing course I took."

"The one where you met your nemesis."

"Right. We'll start talking to men who were sheriffs in counties upriver the year you washed up."

"You said there was a flash flood that year," he said.

"There was. Still, for a baby to survive something like that… it's unlikely."

"But not impossible," he said.

It was getting dark, and she was hearing twigs snap and footsteps every time the wind shifted. The frequency of the sounds convinced her it was just her overly stressed mind and reactivated PTSD, and maybe a little bit of sexual frustration, playing tricks on her perceptions. She glanced at Wolf, and he looked back at her, then frowned.

"You're not okay. What's wrong?"

She shook her head, but he put his hand on her shoulder, urging her to look at him again.

"You can tell me."

"I know I can. But it's stupid and unprofessional, and a distraction from our case."

He blinked. "I was thinking we were more than that. More than PI and client."

She watched his eyes but didn't hold them. Her gaze shifted like a criminal's. "You made it clear you're not interested in that, and I respect your boundaries, Wolf."

He blinked down at her, standing there on the path where it twisted between rock formations and freestanding boulders in striated brown and tan. Beyond them, the sun was setting, striping the sky in gold and orange.

"When did I do that?" he asked. His voice was very soft, barely more than a whisper.

Her darting gaze came back and held on this time. "Well, last night. Obviously."

"Last night I was trying to respect *your* boundaries, Camellia. No means no." He blinked. "Wait, do you mean you've changed your mind about, you know, the old maid thing?"

"What, my draping myself across your chest last night wasn't a big enough clue?"

"Holy... " He peeled his backpack off, dropped it, and caught her face in his hands. Then he tipped it up and kissed her.

She wrapped around him like she was on fire, kissing him back with all the pent-up anguish she'd been keeping inside. They had no tent, no shelter.

He slid his hands down over her backside, her thighs, and lifted them around him, then he carried her off the path while she fed on his jawline, on his ear, on his neck. He dropped to his knees, and when he laid her back on the ground, she shimmied out of her jeans.

He put a hand to her chest, all gentle, slowing her down, his brown eyes asking if she was sure. She peeled her blouse over her head inside out and threw it aside in answer. He did likewise, and then she was done waiting. She pulled him down onto her and into her, closed her eyes, and touched heaven

RANGER DAN, BIG BEND NATIONAL PARK

Ranger Dan was down at the Log-Jam, the watering hole where all the clientele were employees of the park. They kept its existence quiet. Campers looking for a drink and a place to unwind, were directed to a saloon out past the east entrance that was glad to have 'em. This place was their own, only a mile from the north gate.

Dan was starting to feel less than welcome, though. It had become the consensus among his colleagues that he was too old to cut the mustard and ought to retire gracefully. And he supposed they were right, but he didn't have a lot else going on in his life.

He sidled onto a barstool and held up a finger to the bartender, who drew him a glass of his favorite on tap and slid it over without need of instruction, smooth as you please, like they'd rehearsed it.

You had to appreciate the small things like that.

The group of pups, as all the older park staff referred to the youngsters, descended on a table way too close to him, and he decided to seek a spot far from their boisterous, youthful racket. He needed five beers to ease his aching joints enough to sleep, and he'd prefer to enjoy them without the giggling of a bunch of fresh-out-of-braces, empty-headed—he glanced their way, noting the patches on their uniforms—river guides. It figured. Young, fit, cocky, arrogant brats, in his opinion.

River rats, they'd called them back in the day, him and Zach and Billy.

Damn, he missed those guys.

He picked up his beer, having spotted an empty table on the far end of the place, and started past the river rats to get there.

"I'm telling you, it was creepy," said one of them, a girl of twenty-something, dark of hair, eyes, and complexion. The laughter of the others died down. "The way that woman was talking about whether a baby swept into the river could survive to wash up on shore somewhere."

"*Jeeze-iz,*" said another one.

Dan turned around and headed back to his barstool—no, two to the left, nearer the conversation. He didn't want to miss anything.

"Then another one jumps in and says it's for a movie script. They're researching to see if the idea is even viable. But you could tell they came up with that on the spot, you know?"

"Well, what are you saying, Lupe? You think they're gonna dump a real baby into the Rio Grande just to see where it ends up?"

"I think maybe they already did. They were down there by the dumping ground, where the river spews her refuse, doing some kind of ceremony."

Dan spun his barstool around, cleared his throat, and said, "Excuse me."

The girl who'd done most of the talking looked at him, startled, then said, "I'm sorry if we're being too loud."

Huh. Manners from a river rat? Would wonders never cease?

"Not at all," he lied. They were being entirely too loud. It just happened he was glad of it this time. "You don't happen to recall the name of the person asking about a baby in the river, do you?"

"Well, we're not s'posed to share customer info—"

"You're not. I'm a park employee, too."

"Still."

The others with her looked at him as if his age offended them somehow. As if it wasn't going to happen to them, too. Freaking river rats, anyway.

Dan shrugged it off. He could look into yesterday's logbooks as easily as they could. "Never mind, then," he said. "Have a nice evening." And then he headed for the quiet table in the back.

WOLF

He and Camellia didn't really separate the rest of the way back to camp. They walked with every part possible pressed together. Wolf didn't want to let go of her, despite that his brain was trying to break in with logic and warnings. She was clinging close as they walked back, arm in arm. By the time they got to their little campsite, it was late, and his practical mind was getting louder.

This was too much, too soon. She hadn't recovered from her stalker ex, and he'd just lost his mother and his entire identity. This was no time to start a relationship.

But it was kind of late for all that.

He let go of her to crouch and unzip the tent. It felt cold without her in his arms. The sun had set and taken its heat with it. He held the flap open, and she ducked past him inside. He went in behind her, turning around to zip the thing back up, taking his time while she moved around behind him. He had to slow this down, cool it off, use common sense. They'd fallen into each other up there on the trail, and it was time to put their feet back onto the ground.

He finished the zip, rose and turned, and was instantly paralyzed.

She was standing there naked in the orange glow of the portable heater she'd turned on. "I found a fully charged battery in my backpack," she said. She smiled at him in the darkness, then crawled in between the still-zipped-together bags, and crooked her finger at him.

His paralysis fled. He was naked and in there beside her in 3.5 seconds. Once her body slid against his, his irritating common sense shut down for the rest of the night.

Damn, this might be wrong for both of them, but it sure as hell felt right.

CAMELLIA

Camellia had been floating so high in a pink cloud of pheromones and post-coitus endorphins that she'd never even felt her feet touch the ground as they'd walked back to the tent. And then when he took his arm from around her and knelt to unzip it, she'd felt abandoned.

Reason had started to creep back in during that cold moment. He was the first guy to show interest since Earl, and she was still fending off the PTSD, and Wolf was in no frame of mind to be getting involved with anybody.

He was holding the tent flap for her and looking at her with kindness in his eyes. Kindness. Shoot, he was also hearing the voice of reason.

She ducked inside the tent, suddenly feeling the chilly night more than before. Kneeling beside their pile of things, she took out the rechargeable space heater, inserted the battery she'd forget she'd brought along, and turned it on. The thing would run twelve hours on a full charge.

She shed her coat and turned around because Wolf had come inside. His back was to her as he zipped the tent flap closed, moving way slower than seemed warranted. She wasn't ready for common sense to take over between them. Not now, not yet. In the morning, maybe. So she peeled off her clothes and stood there naked when he turned around.

Brave feat accomplished! But standing there was cold, so she crawled into their joined sleeping bags. He shucked his clothes on his way to join her, and his haste made her feel like a love goddess. And then they were all tangled up in each other again. Only this time, he didn't let her lead like he had before. This time, he set the pace, and he set it slow. As he rolled onto his back, pulling her on top of him, Wolf ran his hands over every part of her body while they kissed, like he was committing her to memory. When he followed suit with his lips, she felt worshipped, and their lovemaking lasted long into the night.

WOLF

He didn't think he'd ever felt as warm, as fulfilled, or as relaxed as he did when he fell asleep with Camellia wrapped up in his arms after the most slow, sensual lovemaking he'd ever experienced.

It was powerful, and in its aftermath, he felt changed and couldn't identify how.

That feeling lasted right up until Camellia sat up fast, sucking in a loud breath and letting all the heat out of their love nest. He frowned at her, then he sat up, too. "What's wrong?"

"There's someone outside." She sounded certain.

He crept out of the bag, reaching for his pants and pulling them on, followed by his shirt and hoodie, which he'd removed as one and replaced the same way. He ducked down near their supplies and located the biggest knife they had. "Stay here, okay?"

"Yeah, no." She'd been getting dressed too and was already pulling on her jacket. She grabbed the rubber mallet they'd used to pound in the tent stakes with one hand and a flashlight with the other.

He stepped out, and she came right behind him, her mallet hand resting on his shoulder. She aimed the flashlight beam ahead of them. Something rustled behind the tent, and she swung the light that way fast, but that put her in front of him, and he didn't like that. He moved ahead of her without a lot of caution but held his knife ready. She aimed the light, and he saw motion caught in its beam. Something darted through the thicker woods. Then he tripped and fell across something. Some*one*.

He scrambled up, and Camellia shifted her light, then gasped. "Ranger Dan!"

The old man lay on his back, eyes closed, face lax, and there was blood coming from one side of his head. Kneeling beside him, Wolf checked his pulse in the darkness, because Camellia had moved her light away.

"He's alive," he said. "I need the light, Camellia."

"It was him," she said. "It was Earl. I know it."

Wolf found the ranger's radio on his belt and used it. "Ranger down, ranger down. Campsite um—what is it again, Camellia?" Then to the radio, "Is anyone there?"

The reply came immediately, and Wolf answered questions, keeping his eyes on Camellia as she paced away, aiming her light in the direction of whatever or whoever they'd seen. "It was him," she kept saying. "I know it was him."

"Camellia," he said. "Please, I need the light. Ranger Dan is hurt."

That got her attention. She turned and hurried back, kneeling beside the ranger, aiming the light at the wound in his head. Wolf watched her for a few seconds, trying to see if she was okay. She looked terrified and shocky.

She met his eyes, blinked. "I have a first aid kit in our gear." She tore away so fast she kicked up dirt, and was back five seconds later with the little white kit from her dad's everything-we-need stash. She knelt, opened the kit, and passed him gauze pads.

He tore off the paper wrappers and pressed several layers of pads to the Ranger's bleeding head wound.

Camellia said, "We're here, Dan. You're going to be okay. Help is on the way." She reached for his hand to comfort him, then frowned and said, "He's holding something."

"He's what?"

She pulled a crumbled piece of paper from the old man's clasped hand, smoothed it, and aimed her light at it. "It's a list. Names, addresses, phone numbers, dates... Oh! The dates are all yesterday." She paused a moment. "These are river tour reservations."

"Looks like it was torn from a book," Wolf said when she passed the sheet to him. He was still holding pressure on Dan's head wound with his free hand.

"He was coming to see us, clearly, and he was bringing this," Camellia said. "This is a clue. He must've remembered something or learned something more, and this is related. It has to be."

"But why would anybody bash him over the head about it?" Wolf asked.

"It wasn't about you. I'm telling you, it was Earl. Ranger Dan probably came upon him out there watching our site like the freaking creeper he is."

"Did you get a good look at him, in the woods just now?"

"No," she said and stared into his eyes as if daring him to contradict her. Then the sounds of motors buzzed nearer as four-wheelers' headlamps bounded out of the night and gathered around them.

Camellia snatched the paper from Wolf's hand and quickly folded it into her jacket pocket. Medics with cases gathered around Ranger Dan, and the two of them got out of their way. One, the fellow who seemed to be in charge, asked them what happened.

Camellia said, "I heard something, and it woke me. I think someone hit the ranger with that rock there, near where he fell. We saw someone run off. Or we think that's what we saw. And I think it was my ex-fiancé, Earl Stafford."

The other rangers on the scene looked at her, skepticism in their eyes. "But you didn't see him?"

She shook her head. "No."

Wolf was worried because there'd only been a sudden flurry of motion. It could've been a bird taking flight, or a deer spooking. He hadn't seen anything, and he didn't think Camellia had either. She looked his way, locked eyes with him briefly, then lowered her gaze.

CAMELLIA

Camellia didn't think Wolf believed her. There was worry in his face when he looked at her, not worry that her ex was about to murder her, no. The kind of worried look you give your parent when they repeat the same story three times in a row or put their car keys in the toaster. That look hurt.

Maybe…maybe it had just been physical between them. It had been *really* physical, after all. Boy, had it ever! She got a little tingle every time she thought about it, despite her thorough disappointment in him at the moment.

But she no longer doubted herself and realized she never should have. She had been feeling spiders crawling up and down her spine too frequently to doubt own senses. Earl was here. It'd probably been him following them as they'd hiked up to the shack. Had he seen their frenzied passion on the stony trail and followed them back to discover their campsite, so he could watch her day and night like he had before?

The medics loaded Ranger Dan onto a stretcher and put him onto a small trailer attached to the back of one of the ATVs. Then they drove off to meet an ambulance on the camp road as one ranger questioned Wolf. Another one was still talking to Camellia, but his words were a droning buzz. Her mind was too busy calculating her chances of survival here, in the middle of nowhere, with a companion who didn't believe she was even in danger.

She replied to the questions on autopilot, told the ranger about her ex-stalker and how she'd heard from him again just before this trip, and how she'd seen his Blazer and thought she'd seen him here. She told him all of it, and he didn't take a word of it seriously. She could tell. There wasn't a female ranger among the group. If there had been, maybe things would have been different. But as her mother had been teaching her for her entire life, men don't have clue what it's like to be a woman. They can't understand or empathize. We're like aliens to them.

"He could have fallen, hit his head on that rock there," muttered one of the men near the spot where the old man had been lying.

"Maybe he had a stroke or a heart attack or something," said another. "That could've caused him to fall."

Camellia rolled her eyes. "Am I free to go?" she asked, still on autopilot.

"We don't have anyone registered on this site," said the one in charge. He was lean with gray hair and stern eyes. "Why is that?"

"We were near a cliff, and she sleepwalks," Wolf said. "So we moved to an empty spot and planned to re-register in the morning."

He nodded slow and said, "See to it you do that." Then, to Camellia, "You can go."

She headed back to the tent and felt Wolf's eyes on her but didn't look back. She was on a mission.

Inside the tent, it was too warm. She shut off the little heater and made a mental note to charge its battery at the first opportunity. Then she went to their stack of camping supplies. Most had been unpacked from the giant duffle and arranged in reasonable order. But the extra backpack lay on its side, looking empty.

It wasn't.

She had a gun in that bag, a small but potent .38 caliber revolver with a trigger lock. The key was in the backpack's side pocket.

She'd never been an advocate of guns, but when Earl had been stalking her, she'd decided there were times when a person needed extra protection—especially if that person was a woman with a batshit crazy ex. So she'd bought a gun and taken lessons at a firing range fifteen miles from home. She hadn't even told her mom.

And she hadn't told Wolf that she'd brought the weapon along.

She took the gun out, took off the trigger lock, but turned on the safety. Then she put a bullet into every spot in its revolving chamber. She slid the gun into a pancake holster attached to a wide elastic belt, and then stretched it around her waist under her shirt. Her oversized hoodie covered the gun's bulge.

She was straightening the hoodie when Wolf came in, and she didn't want to talk just then about his belief in her or lack thereof, so she took Ranger Dan's torn sheet of paper out of her pocket and handed it to him.

He studied it. "I know you think this is related to my case, but I can't figure out how."

"Fine, it's not related. We're finished here, then. It'll be daylight soon. Might as well pack up and head home."

"Whoa, whoa, wait, I didn't say it's *not* related. Just that I don't know how."

She rolled her eyes, then crouched low to unzip their sleeping bags, peeling them apart and feeling the symbolism of it like a blade.

"I don't know how either. But why else would he rip this page from a logbook and bring it to our tent in the wee hours, when he wasn't even on duty?"

"How do you know he wasn't on duty?"

"He told us he had to get back and punch out," she said.

"Riiiight." Wolf nodded. "Okay, what if this list *is* a clue? What would we do next?"

"Well, if one of the people who took a boat tour yesterday knows something, then we need to figure out which one, and what they know. We could start following up on these names one by one—what are there, six, seven? Or we could do the obvious thing. Go down by the river and see what that group left under the cairn."

He lowered his head, shaking it slowly. "Come on, Camellia. What are the chances that out of all the parties who booked river tours yesterday, the group we noticed is the one with a connection?"

"What are the chances they're *not*? That woman was Native, Wolf." She held up her hands, like she was balancing platters on each palm. "You *know* I do this for a living, right? You're not doing me a favor by just *pretending* to let me help you, are you Wolf? This is my *job*. And I'm damn good at it."

He stared at her and said nothing. Then he lowered his head and said, "I don't know what I did that has you so pissed at me."

"It's what you didn't do," she said. Then she bit her lip so she wouldn't say more. "And I guess I shouldn't have expected it. Neither of us wanted this."

"Camellia, you're going too fast. I can't keep up."

She couldn't look at him. If she did, she'd cry. "We're breaking camp and getting out of here, but before we head back to the pickup, I'm going down to that spot and looking at what that group left behind. You can do what you want. I was prepaid by my client—your mother—and I'm damn well going to finish the job."

He said, "Okay," and then he turned toward the supplies and started packing them up. After a moment, he asked, "Are you all right, Camellia?"

Just like a man to blame her anger with him on something being wrong with her. She looked him right in the eyes. "Yes. I'm fine. I'm scared, because my stalker is here, and crushingly disappointed that you don't believe me about that."

"Oh," he said, and his face was the human equivalent of a lightbulb turning on.

"Yeah. *Oh.*" She knelt and rolled up the sleeping bags as if she were angry with them, resulting in nice, tight bundles that fit easily into the bag of supplies. Wolf went outside, returning in several trips with the cookstove, its gas tank disconnected, the coffeepot, their folded-up chairs. By the time he'd made the final trip, she had everything else packed in the big canvas bag. She was the only one who knew how to jigsaw puzzle all the parts to fit. Her dad had taught her.

She really missed her dad.

Wolf touched her arm. "I believe you, Camellia. If you say Earl is here, he's here. I'm sorry it took me a minute."

"Or are you just saying that to placate the crazy lady, and make for a peaceful ride home?" She shrugged, shaking her head, hauled the large duffel bag's strap over her shoulder and took it out. Then she set it down and started pulling tent stakes while he was still inside.

CHAPTER ELEVEN

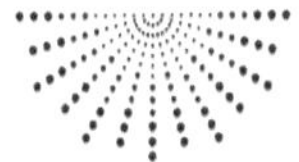

WOLF

The sun rose as they walked, and a tense silence settled over them. Wolf hated it, and he hated feeling so awful, and he missed her being kind of crazy about him.

He said, "Did you know my mom was bipolar?"

He was working things out in his own mind and talking to her about it fresh from there. He had to do something, and telling her how he felt about her wasn't an option—not when he was still figuring that out himself.

Camellia slowed her pace. She'd been speeding along the trail four paces ahead of him, walking off her anger, he hoped. She slowed though and let him catch up. He fell into step beside her. "No. She never told me that."

"I was in middle school when she was diagnosed. I learned what to watch for, you know." They were close to the river, which hummed deep and splashed in the background. "Whenever Ma started saying things that sounded…unlikely, it always meant she was off her meds. It was one of her first signs."

"I'm not bipolar, though."

"I know that. It was just a..." He held up a palm, searching for the word. "Reflex."

Camellia sighed. And then she said, "We're here."

They were. They'd hiked the short distance to where the refuse—what his mom had called river-treasures in her journal—piled up along the riverbank. They walked several yards further upstream, to the finger of ground that made the river bend around it. The little stone cairn the group of paddlers had left stood there still.

It felt like a sacrilege to tamper with the cairn, but Wolf had decided to put absolute faith in Camellia from now on. She'd got him this far, after all. He'd been watching the area around them, especially behind, but there'd been no sign of Earl.

As he knelt at the cairn, he hesitated.

She came and knelt beside him, sliding off her backpack. She said, "I'm super sensitive about not being believed. I think because it was so hard to get anyone to take me seriously about Earl when the stalking started. Even people who knew me got that skeptical look in their eyes. Now that I'm self-analyzing, I realize that's why I had such a rivalry with the second-best student in that PI course I took over the summer. She doubted me. Repeatedly."

Wolf listened to her, really listened and took her words to heart, even though he felt a little sorry for her PI-school nemesis, whoever she was. "I'm not gonna doubt you again, Camellia. That's a promise. Soon as we get a signal, I think we should notify the local police about Earl."

"Yeah, I was gonna do that anyway," she said. But then she smiled at him. "Thank you for believing me. Now let's see what they left here."

He nodded and carefully removed the first few stones until there was room to see inside. "This is probably nothing to do with me," he said, his hand hovering over the opening. "It feels intrusive." It was growing warmer as the sun rose a little higher.

She put a hand over his. "We can put it right back. But we have to be sure."

He looked up and into her blue, blue eyes. They were sparkling. She was excited, certain this was going to be a clue. She was in her element just then, he thought. Lit up, dang near beaming. He looked at her with her peaches-and-cream skin and pink cheeks, from their walk and the warm sun.

And that was when he knew it. He was done. She was *it* for him.

Not knowing Wolf's world had just titled on its axis, Camellia pressed his hand.

He reined in his focus and reached into the little stone volcano to gather up what was there—a small pouch and an envelope. The pouch was brown with a drawstring, and it held some herbs and some stones. He peered inside, then drew it closed again, and turned it over. On the underside, the letters "JWB" had been stitched in blue thread. He traced the letters with his thumb, then he put the pouch back, and opened the envelope carefully. It wasn't sealed. It contained a photograph of a beautiful Native woman in a hospital bed, holding a newborn baby.

Beside him, Camellia gasped, and when he looked at her, she met his eyes and whispered, "Wolf, the bracelet."

He looked at the photo again, at the baby's tiny arm and the brown band tied around his impossibly small wrist. His eyes shot to the woman's face again. She was gazing at the baby with more love than he'd ever seen.

"Wolf, this is your mother," his beautiful companion said.

His eyes welling, he looked at Camellia. She pressed a hand to his cheek. Her eyes were brimming too.

"You did this," he told her. "You're incredible, Camellia, and I—"

Her gaze shifted away from his eyes and a look of stark terror took her face just before something smashed into the back of Wolf's head.

He slammed face-first into the ground, clinging to consciousness.

"No!" Camellia shrieked. "Let go of me! Dammit, Earl, let me go!"

Pushing himself up, Wolf got to his feet and tried to see around the large black spots in his vision. A big man with beach boy looks had Camellia by one arm.

Wolf lunged after them as Earl tried to pull her away with him, toward a canoe beached nearby. There was blood running down Wolf's neck. He felt it as he reached up and grabbed the guy by one shoulder, spun him around, and drove a fist into his chin, then another into his belly.

The guy barely flinched, then he came at Wolf roaring like a bull.

Suddenly, Camellia had a gun in her hand. Wolf saw it, stunned, but Earl didn't—his back was toward her as he hit Wolf so hard his he left ground before smashing down again.

A gunshot rang out. Camellia had fired into the air.

Wolf picked himself up again as Earl surged toward her. He ran after Earl and dove onto the big guy's back, clubbing his ears, but Earl ignored him, focused entirely on Camellia. It was like he couldn't even feel Wolf hitting him.

Camellia was pointing her gun at Earl, while Wolf rode on his back, pummeling him. In a second, Earl grabbed her wrist in a crushing grip, twisting and squeezing.

The gun went off.

Wolf felt like a post-maul hit him. The impact launched him off Earl's back. He hit the ground and he couldn't inhale.

Camellia's screams sounded far away. He looked up as Earl punched her in the head and she dropped to the ground like her bones had dissolved, out cold. He tried to get up, but his body wasn't moving. Only his head, his eyes. He tried to open and close his hands but couldn't tell if they were moving. The sun climbed higher, clearing the rocks and beaming down full force.

Earl threw Camellia over his shoulder and strode away along the riverban, going downstream toward that canoe.

Wolf pushed himself up onto his side as Earl lowered Camellia into the boat, then got in himself and pushed them off from shore.

"Camellia!" Wolf pressed a palm to the ground to push himself upright. But his hand slipped in warm blood and then everything went dark.

WILLOW

Willow had wandered outside with her first cup of coffee, drained it dry and was wishing for a refill. Nothing had come to her overnight. She'd been hoping she'd have a dream or something.

Ethan had found a cell signal a mile away last night, so he was able to reassure himself and get some sleep. He'd driven back to that spot this morning, even before the killer breakfast Orrin and Trevor had cooked up for everyone. He reported back that Lily was still doing fine in his absence.

Willow missed Jeremiah like she'd miss a limb. Maybe she should let the gang off the hook, and the two of them could come back here. Bring Frankie along, camp out in the park. She wondered if dogs the size of small horses were allowed as she walked down across the backyard to the riverbank, where a well-worn trail meandered right alongside. Something compelled her to walk it.

"Will?" Drew called. Because, of course, the little worrywart had followed.

Willow was about to ask for some privacy when sunlight picked out something in the water about a hundred yards further downstream. She frowned, then arched her brows. "Hey, Drew, look where we are!"

Drew looked. "Is that—?"

"The spot with the garbage," Willow said. "What are the odds my friend's cabin would be that close to that spot? I'm telling you, something is—" Her words were cut off by the sound of a gunshot.

Willow froze, her gaze shooting to Drew's.

"You armed?" Drew asked.

Willow shook her head side to side and a second shot rang out. "Get the others," she said and she took off running, leaping roots and boulders, dodging brush and ducking limbs.

A long way down the trail, she spotted someone lying on the ground up ahead, right in the spot where they'd done the ceremony for Wolf. Her heart pounded even harder when the blood on the ground beneath him became visible, too. Racing closer, she saw the man was Native, like her, with sun-kissed brown skin and long black hair.

When Willow finally knelt beside him, she smacked his cheeks, then tore open his shirt and saw that the blood was coming from a hole high on his chest, more like the front of his left shoulder. She asked if he was all right and got no response.

"He's been shot!" she cried, looking up and back, knowing there'd be family on the way.

Her cousins were coming, Drew in the lead, sprinting like a tiny blonde gazelle.

"Is he alive?" Drew shrieked as she landed on her knees near Willow.

"I don't know."

Ethan stopped a couple yards away, and kept his back to her, watching for threats, while the others followed suit, except for

Maria, who arrived several steps behind the others, a small first aid kit in her one hand.

Willow reached for the man's wrist to check for a pulse and saw the dark brown bands of a bracelet tied around it. Her hand stopped moving, and she just stared.

Drew glanced at her. "What is it, Will?"

She snapped to attention, ignoring the insane notion that had briefly crossed her mind. She pressed her fingers to his wrist, felt his strong pulse thrumming. "He's alive." Then she turned his arm to more closely examine the bracelet he wore, just to assure herself that it wasn't, that it couldn't possibly be...

It was the same.

It was the same.

Willow tipped back her head and cut loose a cry that should've summoned every Comanche in the area as her cousins gathered around her, staring at that bracelet and then at the man in absolute wonder.

WOLF

Wolf opened his eyes. There was a woman kneeling over him, holding up his arm by the wrist and keening. She was Native, and she had tears streaming from her eyes when she looked down at him again. He realized there were others around her, but he could only see her.

Why did she look happy? Didn't she know? "He—took her," Wolf managed.

The Native woman's eyebrows bent together. "The man who shot you?"

"He took my...Camellia. On the river." He pointed. God, his chest hurt. He brought a hand to it, but someone pulled it away.

A woman with wild red curls and vivid green eyes said, "Relax, I'm a doctor."

"You're a vet," said a small blonde.

"Well, we left the people-doc back home, so I'm what you've got." The redhead pulled a backpack from her shoulders and started going through it, kneeling on the round opposite the other two.

"The shooter abducted a woman," said the one who'd keened, informing the others. And then, more softly, to him, "I'm Willow."

"Wolf," he said, and she choked on her breath, and he didn't know why. "I have to go after her."

He tried to move the other one's hands away from his chest. She was peeling off his shirt and pressing at the wound, which was higher than he'd thought, and farther left.

"Hit the front of your shoulder," the redhead told him. "A few inches south it'd've been your heart. Looks like the bullet passed right through, which is good. Can you make a fist? Yeah, good. Raise your arm?" She nodded as he did so, though it hurt. "I don't think it hit anything vital. I can patch you up." Then, "This is gonna sting," as she poured what he thought was alcohol over the hole in his body.

There were others, men, four of them, two his age but a lot bigger, two younger and closer to his size. All of them were looking at him with way more in their eyes than *We found a wounded stranger in the woods.*

"I have to go after her," he said again. He was hurting bad.

"That's what any one of us would say in the same situation," said one of the bigger guys, the lighter one. "Go figure."

"We passed some boats back a little ways," the Native woman said. "Orrin, Trevor, go back and get them. Hurry."

"Bring a boat for me," Wolf called, but his voice wasn't very loud.

The Native woman looked at the redheaded animal doctor. "Can he come with us to rescue his, uh…Camellia?"

"Camellia?" the little blonde asked. "Really? That's a pretty unusual name."

"She's a…PI. Helping me."

"You don't say," the little one said. "What's her last name?"

"Rio," he said. "I have to go after her."

"We need to make sure you don't bleed out when you do," said the redhead, pressing bandages over the wound she'd cleaned and taped together. "You move too much, and that bleeding'll start right back up." She closed his shirt.

"I have to go after her." God, it couldn't end like this. Not like this.

Why hadn't he just told her that he loved her? Why hadn't he realized it sooner?

Willow said, "They're coming with the boats." She reached down a hand. He clasped her forearm and she pulled him to his feet. It hurt to move even that much.

He looked where she was looking and saw four canoes in the distance. The younger guys, Orrin and Trevor, were each paddling one and towing another behind.

Willow said, "I know you're going through a lot right now, Wolf." She swallowed hard after saying his name. "But I have to ask—where did you get that bracelet?"

Wolf looked at her again. There was something familiar about her face, but he couldn't put his finger on what. Maybe it was just because she looked like him. He hadn't been raised around many Natives.

He looked toward the boats. They were taking forever. "I was wearing it when my mother found me."

She made a sound like she'd choked on a breath, then swallowed hard and whispered as around her, the others gathered closer, hanging on his words.

"Found you?" Willow asked.

For some reason, he didn't feel like lying. "Yeah, right over there, as a matter of fact. Where the garbage washes up." He just wanted to get the hell out of there and rescue Camellia.

The woman had stopped talking. The canoes were close. He glanced at her, then got stuck on her face, because there were tears sliding over her cheeks. She said, "It seems weird to you we're all so emotional. You see, we're family. Cousins. Close kin. We just found out that my brother was lost in a flash flood before I was born." Her voice was unsteady, broken every now and then by soft breaths. "The river tore him from our mother's arms. He was only two weeks old. And he was...wearing that bracelet."

Everyone around them went silent. The two with the canoes had arrived, pulled their boats up onto the bank, and had come closer to listen in.

Wolf stared at Willow, then at the others, knowing they must be his blood. His family. "What was his name?" he asked, because he didn't know.

"Jonathon Wolf Brand," she said. "My brother."

She slid her arms around his neck and hugged him very gently, and he whispered, "My *sister*?"

And nearby, the littlest blonde muttered, "Camellia freakin' *Rio*. Well, ain't that a kick in the ass!"

CAMELLIA

Camellia fought for consciousness, clawed her way back, and forced her eyes open to look for Wolf. But he wasn't there. He'd been shot with her gun. He'd been on the ground bleeding when Earl had knocked her senseless. All alone, back there. Nobody would find him. He'd bleed to death!

She tried to move her body, to sit up, to turn and look back.

Maybe she could still see him. She pushed herself onto her side, twisting, and the canoe rocked hard.

A dripping wet paddle pressed into the center of her chest. "You stay still now," Earl said. "Don't make me hurt you again."

"I didn't make you hurt me the first time."

"We just need some time, Camellia. That's all we need is some time. You just got confused. You'll come around. I know you will."

"You shot him. You shot him and just left him there." She got herself into a sitting position. Her hands were tied in front of her with a length of rope, and her feet at the ankles with duct tape.

"*I* didn't shoot him," Earl said. "Gun went off. That's not on me."

"Leaving him to die is on you!"

He faced front, because he couldn't look her in the eye, and she knew it.

"Send help back," she pled. "Stop somewhere, anywhere, and tell someone. I won't run away, just—"

"There were folks heading his way," he said. "I heard 'em coming before we left."

"You're lying."

"I'm not." He looked back and met her eyes when he said that.

His eyes weren't right. They were off, not like he was on something, but like the person looking out from behind them was someone else. Someone she didn't know. She said, "You wouldn't do this if you were all right, Earl. Some part of you must know that. Stalking me, kidnapping me, shooting Wolf—"

"I *didn't* shoot him."

"And what about Mary Jo?"

He shook his head. "I didn't do that to Mary Jo. She did it to herself. That's why I'm here, don't you get it? I don't want you to end up like that, too. You women, you get this idea about independence and you can't handle life alone. You're not meant to. You were never designed to be by yourselves."

Something skittered down her spine when he said that. Earl was having some kind of psychotic break, she thought.

"Untie me. Right now, Earl, you pull this boat up and you untie me, or I'll throw myself over the side and drown. I mean it!"

"All right, all right." He set the paddle down and pulled a huge knife from a sheath at his waist. She stiffened and braced when he brought it close, but he only sliced through the duct tape at her ankles. Then he looked up at her wrists and shook his head. "That was a show of good faith. I'll untie your hands after we get a little farther if you behave."

"You can untie them now."

"No, Camellia. You just be thankful I didn't use the zip ties. Cause I could have." He pulled one of the plastic loops out of his pocket to show her. "They're way less comfortable."

"Gee, thanks." She needed to slow him down. If someone had found Wolf, then they'd know by now that she'd been taken. Help could be on the way, and she wanted to give them time to catch up.

"I need to go to the bathroom," she said. "You have to stop."

"No."

"Fine." She turned around as if in a huff, so she was facing backward in the canoe. That way she could watch for rescuers and work on the rope without him seeing. She looked over one shoulder to see him facing forward. The water was picking up speed, so he needed to pay attention to steering them around rocks and such. The idiot didn't even know enough to steer a canoe from the back. She'd be lucky if he didn't capsize it and drown them both.

She started picking at the knots with her teeth, and didn't take long to free her hands. She kept the rope wrapped around them loosely, though.

A slender strand forked off the Rio Grande, and Earl paddled them into it. She watched the main river fall away behind them and looked around for something to leave as a clue. The duct tape he'd cut from her ankles was wadded up in the bottom of the canoe. She quickly tossed a piece of it toward some branches, like leaving a breadcrumb behind.

Ignorant of her actions, Earl paddled into a shallow inlet only a few yards farther, then right up to the shore. He grabbed her arm to help her out of the boat, then pulled the boat behind them with his free hand, until he could tuck it into some dense growth where it wouldn't be seen from the river.

While his back was turned, she tossed the rope from her wrists toward the spot where they'd landed. Then she pulled her hands up under her shirt a little.

"We walk from here," he said.

He couldn't seem to look her in the eyes, as if he knew on some level that he was doing wrong. They hiked into a sparsely wooded no-man's land that was mostly rock and hardpack as the sun blazed down from an ever-higher angle. She wondered how the hell anyone would ever find her. Yanking some hair from her own head when he wasn't watching, she draped the strands over branches at eye level along the trail. She dug her feet into the ground wherever it was soft, ensuring her shoe left an imprint and stomped or stumbled into branches *by accident,* to break their ends off and leave a sign.

She was terrified Earl was going to hurt her or kill her. He was big, which was why it got so scary when he'd become controlling and violent. And she knew of his love for guns. He had hers, now, tucked into the back of his jeans.

He was nothing like Wolf.

God, they'd been so close to finding the answers! The photo in that pile of stones was going to lead them straight to Wolf's birth family. She'd felt it right to her toes.

And the way he'd been looking at her just then, just before the end…

And now, did it even matter? What if Wolf didn't survive? What if he was already gone?

She gulped back a sob, tripped on a stone, and landed on her knees, and then she just let her head fall forward and sobbed. It had been so perfect between them, and then all stupid this morning. Then just when it started to get good again—maybe *really* good—this idiot had to show up and ruin it all.

"Why would you do this to me?" she moaned. "Why did you have to come back and ruin my life all over again?"

He took her by one arm and dragged her to her feet and onward through the wilderness, still not noticing her unbound hands. Or not caring. They moved into a huge ring of rock formations, and then he pulled her into a narrow opening behind one of them.

"What the hell is this? No, we won't even fit back there. What are you—?"

She pulled, but he pulled harder, and instead of bashing into a solid rock wall in the darkness, she was pulled through it into a pitch-dark cave.

"What is this place?" she whispered, but her only answer was the echo of her own voice.

CHAPTER TWELVE

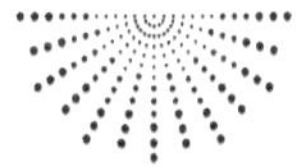

WOLF

olf was in a canoe with the woman who said she was his sister. Willow. He was in the middle of the canoe, facing backward, and she was in the rear, facing him and paddling. As he studied Willow's face against the rising stone walls around them, he realized why she'd seemed familiar before. She looked like him. There was something in her eyebrows, the shape of them, a softer version of his own, and in her nose, too, he thought.

Could it really be true?

"How did you find me?" he asked at length. Of the million questions in his mind, it was the first, and he couldn't make the canoe move any faster, so he might as well use the time to learn more.

"Our parents never told me about you," she said. "Our mother had a complete breakdown after you were swept away. She had to go in-patient for a time, and when she got out, everyone just fell into not talking about you."

"They didn't even search?"

"Oh, they searched. Our uncle Garrett, that's our father's brother, was sheriff. Still is. He hunted for you up and down the river for months. Consulted every police agency along the way, too. Even found your baby blanket, right near that spot where we found you. Which is…" She shook her head slightly, raising her eyes as if looking for spirits in the sky. "Something."

He nodded and resisted the urge to insert questions for more details on every topic. He'd found her. He would have plenty of time to fill in the missing pieces. He wanted to let her speak, because each sentence was a revelation.

"A few weeks ago, looking for something in the attic, I found a cradle with your name engraved on it. I stormed into a family meeting demanding answers. And that's when they finally told us —my cousins and me—the truth. There were old albums full of your baby pictures. You were wearing that bracelet in every one of them."

He twisted his wrist and looked at the bracelet in wonder.

"When Uncle Garrett told me where the blanket was found, I was compelled to find the spot and do a ceremony for you. But really, I wanted to find you or some clue about what had happened to you. And all our cousins came, too. They're all pretty pissed about the lie."

He looked around as she spoke to see them all around him.

"The vet who patched you up is Maria-Michelle, and the little blond aspiring PI is Drew."

"And the big guy with the dark hair is the country singer, Ethan Brand, isn't he?" Wolf asked.

"Yep. We sometimes call him Bubba. He hates it, so we have no choice. And the other big guy with the glasses is Baxter. Drew's brother is Orrin." She pointed at one of the two younger men, the lighter one, then she pointed at his darker counterpart and said, "And that's Trevor."

He said, "I saw your ceremony. That was for me?"

"That was you? Up on the cliffs? I thought I was seeing your spirit."

"You were, cuz," called the little blonde, Drew, from the nearby canoe she shared with the vet, Maria. "It was just still in his body at the time." Laughter floated over the water.

Ethan Brand said, "We're glad we found you, Wolf."

"So glad" was echoed by many voices.

"I can hardly believe this is real," Ethan went on, then he sent a look Willow's way. "Sorry I doubted you, cuz."

The redhead in the boat with Drew said, "Hold up, hold up!" And everyone back-paddled or moved to one side out of the current. There was a fork where a small tributary veered off. The redhead padded into it real slow, looking around with care, then said, "This way!"

Nobody even questioned her; they all just followed. Wolf said, "She's a veterinarian?"

"Her mamma is our dad's baby sister, Jessi, and she can track like nobody's business. Taught Maria how."

"And Ethan's my cousin, too?"

"Yes, he was adopted though. Found on the doorstep as a baby."

He looked at her wide-eyed.

"Don't worry, brother. I'll catch you up on the family history once we rescue your lady fair."

He felt his face heat, lowered his eyes, then looked up again, unable to stop asking questions. "What about our parents?"

"Their names are Wes and Taylor, and they are going to lose their freakin' minds when we find a way to tell them." Then she said louder, "How should we tell Mom and Dad? Should I call when we get a signal?"

"Let's get Camellia back before we worry about that, huh?" Drew asked.

Up ahead, Maria had plucked a piece of duct tape from some branches along the water's edge. Turning back, she held up a finger for quiet, then pointed to her eyes, and swept her hand in a wide arc.

He went very quiet and started watching the shoreline for any sign of Camellia. Willow was watching the left side, so he focused on the right. The only sounds were the gentle dips of paddles, and the dripping of water from their edges when they rose again. The sun was cooler in this wooded strand where branches caused its light to dapple the water.

Willow asked softly, "What happened to you, Wolf? How did you survive? Where have you been all this time?"

"It's a long story," he said. "And I don't know how I survived the river. I only know I was found in the water by a girl. Fourteen. A runaway and a survivor. She raised me as her own. I didn't know the truth until she told me on her deathbed a couple weeks ago."

"Oh, God, you just lost your mom?"

He nodded. "And found my sister."

"All that in a couple of weeks? And now this." Then she blinked. "I'm not being a very good cop—"

"You're a *cop*?"

"Deputy," she said, keeping her voice low and her eyes on the shoreline. "Who is this guy who took your friend? Do you know?"

He nodded. "Earl Stafford. Her ex. He turned stalker after she broke up with him three years ago. But she said he'd been getting weird before that. Controlling and suspicious. Got in with some bad people, she thought. He stalked her and only stopped six months ago when he got a new girlfriend. That one took her own life, and he started up again with Camellia."

Ahead of them, Maria, the redhead, raised a hand in the air, then pointed. He saw a small piece of rope on the shore, and then spotted the ass-end of a canoe sticking out of some thick brush near the shore.

They beached their canoes, dragging them up out of the water as the little blonde raced ahead of the others to look at the boat.

She looked inside, then called back to them, "Camellia scratched her initials into the side, that clever little snoop."

Willow went for a closer look as well but didn't seem to find any additional clues. Maria called, "This way," in a stage whisper.

Wolf walked up front with Willow and Maria, who skimmed the surroundings with her hawklike gaze, missing nothing. Seven people surrounded him, just like family. Maria found pieces of Camellia's glorious hair, and footprints in the dirt, and broken branches. She said, "She's leaving a trail for us."

"Always was about as clever as a G.D. fox," Drew said.

Wolf looked at her frowning, because it wasn't her first odd comment about Camellia, but before he could ask, she said, "Full disclosure. I know her from PI school."

And it clicked in his mind. "You're her *nemesis*," he said as he realized.

"She found out I was named after Nancy Drew and never let me hear the end of it," she replied. "We competed *hard* in that class. Had to, since nobody else held a candle to either of us." Then she shrugged. "Made each other better, I guess."

She stomped ahead, but then she stopped short and dropped suddenly to her knees, motioning behind her with one arm for them all to do the same. "There's a shoe over there where a shoe shouldn't be," she said.

Everyone hunkered down, inching closer.

Sure enough, in a cluster of large boulders and formations, one of Camellia's walking shoes lay on its side. He started to panic, but the little blonde put a hand on his shoulder and said, "Don't go thinking something bad happened. She's been leaving us a trail. She must've run outta things to drop."

"It's all open in the center of that cluster," Maria said, gazing at the rock formations that towered high around it. "Good spot to get ambushed."

"Let's move around this outcropping," Ethan said. "See if we can pick up their trail on the other side. Be quiet, though. They could be close."

They crept around the boulders, moving inland from the river bank several hundred feet, as the formations were huge and sprawling. Wolf watched the ground for signs, footprints, anything along the way, but the ground was pristine. Camellia and Earl had clearly go through the cluster, not around the outside.

On the far side of the formation, there wasn't a clue anyone had come out, though, and in fact, the boulders on this side were a solid wall. There was only one way in or out of the cluster, back around the side where they'd found the shoe.

"They're in that cluster somewhere," said Maria-Michelle.

"We have to assume he's armed," Willow added. "The gun that shot Wolf wasn't anywhere at the scene." She peered through a crevice into the cluster of boulders. "He could be behind any one of those rocks, waitin' in ambush. We should climb up top, get a better view."

"Screw that," Wolf said. He broke away from the others, ran back around the boulders and went through the only opening into the large cluster of stones toward Camellia's shoe. Running footsteps followed. About four steps in, he felt something across his shin, and the words "trip wire" rang in his mind far louder than the firecracker sound that came from above. He looked up and saw boulders plummeting.

CAMELLIA

Earl was pulling her along by her upper arm, deeper and deeper into the cave, but when she heard what sounded like a gunshots or small explosions, she jerked her arm free and started running back the way they'd come through pitch darkness with her arms out in front of her so she wouldn't hit a wall.

Earl swore, caught her in two strides, and pulled her back. There was a roar and pounding outside.

"Is it a cave-in?" she almost shrieked.

"It's a welcome I left for anyone who tries to come this way," he said. "Seems like your boyfriend wasn't hurt too bad after all."

"Anyone could have wandered this way, you idiot." He was pulling her again. She heeled off her remaining shoe and left it behind, limping along in her socks. She was running out of breadcrumbs to leave.

"You don't understand," Earl said. "You don't know how things really are, but you'll see. I'll show you and then you'll understand. I can't let you die like Mary Jo."

He wasn't okay. In fact, she was pretty sure he was the farthest thing from okay and probably in desperate need of medical intervention. "Where are we going, Earl?"

"A safe place. A safe place."

"A safe place in a cave?" They seemed to be moving deeper into the earth. She'd lost all sense of direction, couldn't judge which way they were going, other than down. The ground was definitely sloping downward. But eventually, it felt as if it was sloping upward again. When a sliver of light appeared up ahead, relief washed over Camellia at the sight. At least he wasn't going to kill her in the dark.

He pulled her along toward the light, which grew into a tall, narrow crack in a solid stone face. They moved through it, its space so tight the cold stone touched her shoulders. When she stepped out into the hot sun, it warmed the cave's chill right out of her, and she could hear the reassuring sound of the Rio Grande nearby. They hadn't gone too far, then.

They were standing in front of a square structure whose top and sides were made of rusted steel roofing. One section of it was hinged and held in place by a rope looped around a peg—a makeshift door. She looked around the place, saw nobody else nearby. There was a row of targets lined up off to the left—and pieces of tin with bullseyes painted crookedly, all full of holes. There was a four-foot-tall tank on legs with a spigot on the front. Water, she guessed. She looked around and then realized that the sound of the river wasn't coming from where it should, and when she spotted it, it seemed the water was flowing the wrong way.

"Wait, wait a minute here. Are we in Mexico?"

"Like I said, a safe place where nobody's gonna bother us."

"Yeah, no."

She pulled away again, but he grabbed her, threw her over his shoulder, and walked along a narrow path toward the shack amid junk of every imaginable sort as she twisted and thrashed, he stopped all at once and said, "Be still!"

The tone startled her so much she stopped moving.

"You move we both die," he said, "I'm not kidding around."

For some reason she believed him, so stayed still while he took her inside and put her down on her feet. The place was a dump, with ratty overstuffed chairs, a kitchen-style table completely covered in bullets, casings, gunpowder, reloading equipment, and other stuff she couldn't have named. There were random tools everywhere she looked.

"This one of the places you go with your group?" she asked.

He pushed her into one of the chairs, and she was sure there were creatures of some kind nesting in it. Then he walked away. As soon as he did, she got up and lunged for the door. She had hold of its rope handle when he came up, bent low, and grabbed her by her ankle. He yanked her leg right out from under her. She fell face down on the floor and he dragged her back to the chair, bending to pick up a shackle attached to a bolted-down chain.

She panicked. "No. No. No." She kicked with her other foot but he acted like he didn't even feel it and snapped the metal band around her ankle, though she fought. When the lock snapped, she kicked him right in the face and felt his nose crack under her heel. Blood exploded from his nose, and he staggered backward and fell on the floor.

She scrambled to her feet, grabbed the chain attached to her shackle, and yanked hard. It didn't budge, so she started working on the lock, but that was no good either.

Earl got up, hand to his bleeding nose. He walked away like he was no longer worried she might escape, and when he came back, he had a wet rag on his nose and a thick folder in his other hand.

"Here," he said, and he dropped the folder onto the little table beside the probably rodent-infested chair. "Read it. The whole thing. Then you can go."

She blinked in shock. "That's all you want? For me to read this?"

"Once you do, you'll change your mind. So yeah, that's all I want."

"You shot Wolf—"

"I did not!"

"—and kidnapped me just to make me read this?" she said. "Earl, you're not okay right now. You need help."

"What I need is for you to read the manifesto."

She blinked at the word, and realized he was further gone than she'd even suspected.

"Read it!"

"Okay, okay." She kicked the chair twice, hoping to scare out any residents, sat down, and picked up the folder.

WOLF

As the avalanche of boulders descended on Wolf, something else hit him first. The big guy, Ethan Brand, in a kind of flying leap, took him out of the path of those boulders and onto the ground, where he landed on top of him. It hurt like hell.

Ethan got up as the final few rocks fell behind him, forming a neat pile where Wolf had been standing. From amid a cloud of deep brown dust, his cousin reached down a hand. Wolf clasped hold and was pulled to his feet.

"Thanks."

"*De nada*," Ethan said. You okay?"

Wolf put a hand on the front of his bandaged shoulder. From beneath the shirt and bandages, fresh blood warmed his hand. "I'm good." Then he looked around as the others joined them.

"We'll have to watch for booby traps from here on," Ethan said.

Willow came and clapped Wolf's uninjured shoulder. "That means we're close."

"Yeah, but where are they?" Maria asked, skimming the area.

"I'd say they went that-away," Drew all but sang, and when Wolf followed where she was pointing, he saw the dark shadow between two boulders and realized it was a cave.

"Let's go." He headed for the entrance

"Slowly," Willow said. "Watch for booby traps."

"Booty taps," Baxter said, but his chuckle cut off when nobody appeared to get his joke. "What? Nobody saw *Goonies*?"

"Use references from the current century, cuz," Drew said.

Wolf slowed his pace, made himself check carefully before each step, and yet going slow was the last thing he wanted to do. He used his phone for a flashlight, aiming the beam in every direction around him as he led this team of newfound kinfolk deeper into trouble.

Maybe his ma had picked the right surname, after all.

"Are you absolutely sure they went this way?" Willow asked.

"They came in here," Maria said. "They left clear footprints near the entrance."

"Then where did they go?" Willow whispered.

Wolf's light fell on something. He hurried to retrieve it. "It's Camellia's other shoe." He held it up.

Eventually, they emerged from the cave and into blinding sunlight and their goal—a rusty tin shack with targets set up to the left, no trespassing signs all around, and a junkyard for a dooryard.

"Okay," Willow said, crouching low. "We haven't found another booby trap yet, but up near that place, I can see three from here, and I haven't even got around to looking very hard." She pointed. "He has hand grenades hidden like easter eggs along the path to the front door."

Wolf looked where she pointed. One was duct taped to an old metal birdbath, another to a discarded toaster just lying on the ground. Each had a string through the loop of its pin, which led to a trip line in the path. If you tripped the line, it pulled the pin, and three seconds later something near you exploded.

"Camellia said Earl got with a group of radicals. All about guns and survivalist shit. Said they went all over the state for what they called training weekends. Described sites like this."

Willow sighed. "Does anybody have a cell signal?"

A lot of checking was followed by a murmur of nopes.

"I'm going around the back," Wolf said. Willow moved with him. They gave the place a wide berth, circling it while staying behind boulders, brush, rusty barrels, and those crooked targets.

They reached the back of the place. No windows, no openings, no way to see inside, and the thought of what the brute might be doing to Camellia was torture. But the place was silent. Not a sound came from within. There was a door in the back, if you could call it a door. It was the same as the one in the front, a cut out section of the tin-sided wonder with a rope through it.

This one's hinges were strips of rubber nailed to the frame on one side.

"I don't see any trip wires this time," Willow said. She took a step forward. The ground cracked open and she dropped into it.

Wolf lunged, caught her forearm, and held tight. She looked up at him and smiled. He smiled back, but it died when he looked past her and saw spikes in the bottom of the grave-sized hole in the ground. The hole had been covered with a paper-thin layer of pre-cracked plywood, which was then scattered with pebbles and dirt to make it look like the ground.

He pulled her out before her cousins could even make their way in to help. When she was on solid ground again, they both examined the garbage strewn between them and the building ten yards away, realizing that every scrap in the yard and the yard itself were potential death traps.

Wolf wanted to roar in frustration. To be this close to Camellia and unable to see her, to even know if she was okay, much less get to her—it was maddening. And his damn wound was bleeding more than before.

Camellia

"There's something alive in this chair," Camellia said, having determined that there probably wasn't. Still, she slid out of the chair and onto the floor, sitting so that her knee blocked Earl's view of the place where the chain was bolted to the floor. She started scraping at the wooden floor around the bolt with her fingernails, whenever he wasn't looking.

She tried to read some of the pages of his manifesto, but there were eighty-two of them, single spaced, and so far, it was one long run-on sentence, written with extreme urgency and zero logic. She recognized the themes of a few Q-anon theories, but they'd been enhanced and embroidered with tales of his own about how birth control pills were controlling the minds of women, which explained why they wanted careers and independence instead of the comfort and security inherent under the guardianship and rule of men.

Obviously, she was supposed to see the error of her ways and throw herself on his mercy. So she skimmed, taking a long time to turn each page, peeling away a splinter of floor at a time. It was taking too long, however, and she looked for another option. There were tools tossed around the place every which way, and after a bit, she noticed a crowbar in the corner. She got up to her feet, and paced while she read, to see how far she could reach. It caught his attention, and he looked up at her, watched her, but she pretended not to even notice and just kept pacing back and forth, her eyes glued to his pages. Her chain didn't reach the crowbar, but if she could lie down and extend her arms all the way, she might.

A bell jingled violently, and she dang near jumped out of her skin. "What the hell was that?"

"Hehehe. Somebody fell in the pit."

"The pit?"

"Spikes in the bottom. Nothing survives the pit. I tell you, this place is impenetrable."

"This place is *Home Alone* on a fifty-dollar budget." She said it before she could stop herself. Then she threw the folder back toward the chair she didn't want to sit in. "I'm not reading another word till you go out and check and tell me who you just killed."

"I didn't kill anybody. There's signs everywhere. If you walk past a no trespassing sign, I'm within my rights to—"

"I don't give a shit about your rights. Get out there and tell me who's in your pit, or I'll shred that manifesto instead of reading it."

"All right, all right." He went to the back door, rather than the front. She had not spotted it, so it was helpful to know it was there. He stepped out and closed it behind him, so she couldn't see outside. No matter, she had to move fast.

She went as far as the chain would reach, then laid on her front and stretched her arm until her fingertips brushed against the crowbar. She scrambled them against it, but she couldn't get a hold on it.

Then genius struck. She yanked out her jade hairpin and used it to extend her reach. She pulled the bar the slightest bit closer with the hairpin, then grabbed it in her hand, ran back to the spot where the chain was bolted down, and pried. The bolt in the floor rose a little. She pulled the crowbar back and jammed it in, pried again, and the bolt rose a little more. One more try. She removed the bar, jammed it even deeper into the floor, and pried.

The entire bolt popped out of the floor, with its nut still attached on the other end, tearing the wood as it came free. Good.

Earl was coming back, opening that door. She kept the crowbar in her hand, grabbed her jade hair pin, and ran to the door carrying the chain so it wouldn't rattle. Then she stood just inside. When Earl stepped back through it, she swung the bar like Alex Rodriguez swings a bat, hit Earl upside the head as hard as she could, and hoped it wouldn't kill him. She didn't want him dead, but she wasn't holding back.

He went down in a heap. She jumped over him, still clutching the crowbar as she lunged out the door, he wailed, getting up again, two steps behind her. "Camellia, no! You'll die like Mary Jo did!"

She spun around, so startled by him bellowing from right behind her that she whipped the crowbar. It nailed him right between the eyes, and he dropped.

He stayed down that time.

CHAPTER THIRTEEN

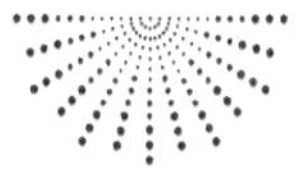

Wolf

While Wolf was still figuring out how to get to Camellia, the back door opened, and Earl—who was bigger than Ethan or Baxter Brand—stepped out. Wolf and his newfound kin were all ducking low. It was easy to hide behind the refuse pile that surrounded the place.

"Wish I'd brought my gun," Willow muttered.

Earl looked around, stood on tiptoe, his gaze aimed at the pit that had almost claimed Willow. Then he reached beside the door to grab a pair of binoculars.

"Can you rope him, Trevor?" Maria asked.

Rope him? Wolf wondered. What kind of family was this?

Trevor shook his dark, curly head. "Too much junk in the way."

"He's going back inside. Throw a rock or something," Drew whispered.

Her brother Orrin picked up a rock, rose, and wound up for

the pitch. And then there was a thud, and the big guy sank to the floor.

And then Camellia, stepped over him. Her hair was loose and wild around her shoulders. She wore no shoes and one sock, held a crowbar in one hand and something smaller in the other.

The Brands rose from their cover, but Earl rose, too, before Camellia had gone two feet from the door, and he yelled at her to stop. She spun and whipped that crowbar hard.

Earl went down in a heap. Camellia stared at him for a moment, and then turned, gathered up all her hair, and did that twist, flip, twist thing she did and stabbed her hairpin into it. That was what she'd had in her other hand.

He was smiling and shaking his head at her when she finally met his eyes. Her face lit up, and she lunged forward, and every single hand around Wolf flew up, stop-sign style, as every voice chorused some version of, "No, don't move" or "Stay where you are."

Camellia froze in place, glancing over her shoulder. Earl hadn't moved, but he might, and Wolf could almost feel the shivers running up and down Camellia's spine at having that big asshole so close behind her.

"I really need to come out there, Wolf."

"I know. It's booby-trapped. Let me come to you."

"So it's not booby-trapped for you, then?"

Something banged on the roof, startling Camellia so badly she jumped. Then she pivoted and looked up where the rest of them were already looking, at little blonde Drew. She'd apparently jumped down from the rock formation above, and had landed in superhero pose on the rusty roof.

CAMELIA

"Nancy freaking Drew," Camellia said to her slightly built, blond-ponytailed nemesis. "How in the hell are you here?"

"You win," Drew said, extending a hand.

"Excuse me, but aren't you the one rescuing me right now?" Camellia took her hand, stepped up onto a barrel, and then onto the roof with Drew's help.

"Yeah, true. *But* we were both on the same case. You found my cousin before I did."

"I wasn't looking for your cousin. I was looking for his family. Wait, *cousin?*"

"And we're a tight family, too." They walked across the roof and climbed up onto the boulder that stood above it. Drew boosted her up, then Camellia reached back to pull her up in return. "It would be something if we wound up related," Drew said. Then she crooked an eyebrow. "How close are you two?"

"Not as close as I want us to be," Camellia muttered.

"Ohhh, I wouldn't be too sure about that," Drew said, glancing back at the group.

Camellia figured they were all kin, but she only had eyes for Wolf. He was gazing back at her, and it felt like he was already holding her in his arms, just from the look in his eyes. The shirt he wore was torn and bloody, but he was on his feet and appeared to be okay. She and Drew jumped from boulder to boulder until they could climb down clear of Earl's booby traps, and then she ran right into Wolf's arms.

He grunted when she hit him but held her close, "Thank God you're okay," he said.

"Thank God you are," she said back, her face buried near his neck as he held her. "Wolf, I realized something back there, when you were shot. I—"

He wasn't hugging her back anymore, and there was dampness forming between his chest and hers.

"Wolf?"

He sank to the ground. "No! Nonononono, Wolf."

A woman with red curls came quickly and knelt beside him. "He's bleeding again." Then she looked behind them. "We need to get him out of here. He needs blood, but I don't think he's going to die."

"Mmm-nah-gone-die," Wolf muttered, sitting up.

Drew said, "Wait, wait, my phone vibrated when we were crossing the boulders. There must be a signal up there."

"I've got it," said a big man with dark hair, who reminded Camellia of a country singer whose name she couldn't recall. He climbed up onto the rocks, holding his phone high.

And the Native woman said, "Wait, where's Earl?"

For Camellia, it unfolded in slow motion, even though it was happening at high speed. She rose and turned, chills racing up and down her spine again, and Earl was running at her like a bull. His eyes were fixed on hers as if he didn't even see anyone else. He crossed the junk-strewn yard, leaping from one spot to the next to avoid his own traps, like a gorilla doing parkour. The final leap would bring him right down on her, and there wasn't even time to move.

Wolf surged to his feet, bringing his fist with him in an uppercut as Earl descended. The big man's head snapped back, and Wolf's other fist smashed him in the face. Then wolf sagged and Camellia caught him in her arms. Earl had flipped backward into the waiting arms of a large golden-haired man with eyeglasses, who said, "Trevor, you got that rope?"

"Can't bind him with a lasso, cuz. That's not how they work," she a younger man.

"That's okay," Camellia said. "He has zip ties in his pockets." She was easing Wolf back down. He wore a goofy smile and was feeling no pain.

Ethan had been ready to jump in from his perch atop the boulders, but now he turned and held up his phone. "Got a bar," he announced. "I'll get a chopper in here for Wolf and—oh Lord! *Oh Lord!*"

"Bubba, for God's sake, what?" the redhead cried.

"Lily's in labor!" the big guy shouted.

"Drew, you'd best take over the phone calls," said a the Native woman, as Camellia realized she looked an awful lot like Wolf....

The woman noticed her looking and smiled. "I'm Willow. I'm his sister," she said.

Her nemesis-turned-rescuer, Nancy Drew, climbed the rock, and Willow called out, "Don't tell the family about Wolf. Not on the phone. I need to be more careful with Mom this time."

Everyone murmured in agreement.

WOLF

God, they were beautiful, the couple who stood on their home's front porch as Willow drove them into the driveway, in her pickup truck.

Wolf had received two units of blood and had been patched up. Ethan and Lily had been sent home from the same hospital in El Paso with a diagnosis of false labor. Nobody, other than the cousins, had been told about Wolf yet.

Willow stopped the truck. She said, "Okay, here we go." And she got out, and Wolf got out.

"I shouldn't be here," Camellia said.

"Yes, you should," Wolf told her. "Camellia, I...there's so much."

"I know," she said. "Same." Their eyes held, and he nodded, understanding. There hadn't been a minute to discuss what was between them since he'd awakened in the hospital.

"Soon, though," he promised.

He got out, held the door for her. Willow was already approaching the front porch. He felt awkward and uneasy as he studied the couple from a distance. Native, both of them. The mother—*his* mother, Taylor Brand—was an older version of his sister, though Willow had her father's brow and jawline. So did he.

"Hi, Mom, Dad," Willow called.

"Welcome home, honey. Who's that you've brought with you?" their mother asked. Their father, Wes Brand, was leaning forward in his chair, his eyes narrowing on Wolf.

"Mom, something miraculous happened when we went to the place where my brother's baby blanket was found," Willow said.

"You...went there?" Taylor looked stunned, and sent her eyes to her husband, but they returned to Willow's when she spoke again.

"Yes. We held a ceremony for him. But...then we learned about a baby boy who was found in the river—"

Their mother rose to her feet, her sharp gasp stopping Willow only briefly.

"It's okay, Mom. He was found *alive*, washed up on shore. He was raised by women who were off the grid by necessity."

"Are you saying...Willow are telling me my son is alive?" she asked, but the words were mostly air. She seemed to wobble on her feet a little, and her husband's arm tightened around her shoulders.

"Willow, if you're not sure about this," their father warned.

What a man he was, Wolf thought, watching his jaw clench as he held his wife nearer, as if he'd protect her from harm with his own body if he had to.

"Wolf is alive, and he's okay, Dad. And...we brought him home. He's right here." And she turned to look at him.

The eyes of his parents turned toward him. He walked closer, still clinging to Camellia's hand. The woman—his mother—released a strangled sob. Her face was soft, her mouth open, her brows so arched her forehead was an accordion. "Wolf?"

"That's...what my bracelet says." He raised his hand, loosely fisted, to show what he wore on his wrist.

She gasped, one hand covering her mouth. Then she launched

from her husband's arms and wrapped her arms around him. It hurt like hell and he didn't care at all. She kept saying his name over and over in a way he'd never heard it before. "Johnny Wolf, my Johnny Wolf," she said while stroking his head. Eventually she backed up just a little, clasping his face between her hands and gazing up at him.

Her husband appeared behind her, his hands on her shoulders, his discerning brown eyes on Wolf's face. "Son?" he croaked.

"You look like your father," whispered his mother.

And then the man's eyes closed, and his head dropped backward and he said, "Thankyouthankyouthankyouthankyouthankyou."

CAMELLIA

Camellia still felt out of place as they had dinner around a big dining table in the home of Wolf's parents, Wes and Taylor Brand, on Sky Dancer Ranch, where they raised, boarded, and trained horses.

Willow and her fiancé, Jeremiah, whom she frequently called Gringo, had sat on one side of the table with their nine-year-old Frankie between them. Camellia and Wolf sat on the other side, with the parents at either end. Wes and Taylor couldn't stop looking at Wolf, and Camellia could feel it was making him a little uneasy.

"Earl's been arrested," Willow said, "but they moved him to a psych unit until they can get him stabilized." She'd already filled everyone in on what had happened at Big Bend, keeping the scarier parts to the adults only. "That's a national park, which makes his crimes federal. But a lot will depend on his diagnosis." She nodded to Camellia. "I gave them your Detective Simms' contact info like you asked, told them about his recent girlfriend."

"I think his mental health has been declining for a while, and his girlfriend's death pushed him over the edge," Camellia said. "I'm glad he's getting help."

Wolf said, "Have you spoken to your mom, Camellia?"

"I have. She wants to come down and meet you all."

"We'd love that," Taylor said. "She's up in Hobbsville, you mentioned?"

"For now, but she's just decided to put the house on the market, so who knows? We've both been feeling the lure if greener pastures."

"Maybe she'll like it here and want to stay," Taylor said with a glance at her husband. "Not exactly greener, but it does seem to happen to a lot of folks."

"Happened to you," said Wes, sliding his hand across hers on the table.

Camellia looked at Wolf. He was looking back at her. There was so much unresolved between them, and she was dying for some alone time with him. But he needed this time with his family first.

"I really would be happy to go to a hotel," she said at length, and not for the first time. "You all need time as a family."

Willow said, "There *is* no hotel, unless you count the rooms over the saloon. Boarding house is even closed now."

"Even if you wanted to go, there's no need," said her mother, Taylor. "Willow's cottage has been empty since she and Jeremiah bought a place together. It's just a little farther along the driveway, and you're welcome to use it Camellia."

"That sounds nice," she replied.

"There's a bedroom and a hideaway sofa-bed," Willow said with a knowing look at her brother. "You can both spend the night out there. Process some of this. A lot's happened today."

"Oh," said Taylor, and there was disappointment in her tone, but she tried to cover it. "Yes, sure, that's a perfect idea. This must be…overwhelming for you, after all you've been through."

"It is a little," Wolf admitted.

"We'll pack you up some supplies, bedding and snacks and things," she said.

"That would be really great." Wolf spoke softly, watching his birth mother's face and looking as everyone rose and migrated out onto the front porch.

Camellia said, "We could all have breakfast together though, and spend the morning just…talking."

They'd done quite a lot of talking already tonight, and Camellia felt like the healing was almost visible to the naked eye.

Taylor brightened. "I'd love that, and I'll count the hours. But there's no need to rush. We have time now." She looked at her son. "We lost a lot, but we have time now. I never thought we would." She leaned up and kissed his cheek, and Wolf's eyes got wet. "I'll see you in the morning, son," his mother told him.

Then she turned to Camellia, and reaching up, touched her face. "Good night, Camellia. There are no words to thank you for bringing him back to us. I hope you can feel—"

"I can," she whispered. "I do."

WOLF

It had been a long, long day.

Wolf was sitting on the small front porch of what his mother had called Willow's cottage. Willow had texted to let him know Ranger Dan was awake and he was going to be all right.

There were rocking chairs on either side of the small cottage's front door, and he sat in one of them. Camellia was taking a shower.

The poor thing had offered to go to a hotel so many times he was beginning to feel like his family was holding her against her will. But he didn't want her to go.

He sat there, feeling the cool, dry air of a West Texas night on his face. Horses grazed in a nearby meadow, and the scent of horseflesh was on every breeze. This was Brand land, his father had told him, as far as the eye could see. And he was a Brand. Wes and Taylor's ranch butted up against the Texas Brand, where his father had been raised, where cattle still grazed.

From the outside, he'd have thought this family had it easy. But he'd seen the pain in his mother's eyes when she'd said she was sorry for letting the river take him from her arms. And even though he was okay and had somehow found his way back to her, he didn't think she'd ever get over it.

He'd carried in the four boxes his parents had packed hastily, bedding, food, bathroom supplies, and so on. There was a digital clock and a card with the internet password on it. He'd already unpacked most of it.

Eventually, he heard the creak of the screen door and felt Camellia's soft footsteps on the porch. She was barefoot.

He didn't look up until something cold touched his check. A dewy brown longneck already opened. He took it and sent her a smile. "Do you really want a hotel?" he asked.

"I just didn't want to get in the way of such a personal time for you."

He nodded. "I don't know that I would've got through it without you there, though."

"Really?"

She sounded skeptical, but her back was to him as she walked to the other rocking chair, twisting off her bottle cap on the way.

"You couldn't tell by how tight I've been holding onto you?" he asked.

She smiled, then took a big pull from her bottle.

"I'm glad you stayed, though," he said. "I wanted…to ask you something."

"Ask away." She took another drink.

She was nervous, he thought, and trying to cover it. "Well, before, you said you'd realized something when I was shot. But you never said what. Or maybe you did, but I didn't hear it, being unconscious and all."

Nodding slowly, she took a long, thoughtful sip of beer. "What I realized was that I might not *want* to be ready for a relationship, but I am anyway. Like it or not."

And he said, "Same."

"Oh, I see how this is going down. I have to say all the hard stuff and you get to just say same?"

"Ditto?" he asked.

Then he got up, set his beer on the railing, and moved to the front of her chair. "I'm not ready for a relationship with anyone else but you," he said, threading his fingers through hers, both hands, and pulling her to her feet. "But *with* you," he went on, "I'm not ready for anything but. I want you in my life."

"I want that, too," she whispered.

And he went on, because he was worried. "And I think I want that life to be here, where my family is," he said.

She smiled, lowering her head. "I didn't want to be presumptuous, but when I spoke to Mom, I mentioned that…if things worked out for us, I might end up living in West Texas. That's why she's *really* driving down here after her cruise, to check things out. And she's gonna *love* your family."

"Everybody loves my family, apparently."

She took a deep breath. "Drew asked if I'd be interested in teaming up with her, hanging up our shingle as PIs together. Says she needs a partner."

Camellia had really been thinking about this, then. That must mean her feelings were strong. As strong as his? Man, he was starting to feel ten feet tall.

"What will *you* do here, Wolf?" she asked.

"My father offered to hire me on here at the ranch. I told him my skills are in building. I'll check some of the local construction crews, I imagine."

She said, "I thought you died, you know. When he shot you, I thought…"

He caught her chin and tipped it up and kissed her mouth and then kissed it some more. Fire rekindled, having never been banked, and when his mouth slid from hers to her jaw, to her neck, and into that tender hollow just behind her ear, words slid from his lips as if on their own.

"I love you, Camellia Rio. I love you, I love you, I love you, and I waited way too long to say it." And then he kissed her lips again.

Her mouth curved into a smile against his as she whispered on a sigh, "Same."

EPILOGUE

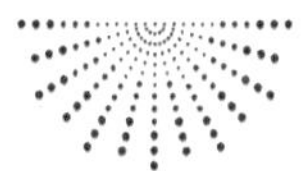

WOLF

The next afternoon, after a glorious morning with his parents, Wolf and Camellia drove Wolf's rusty, trusty Ford truck over a long dirt road, beneath a big wooden arch with the words "TeXas Brand" cut out of it. The ranch house spread wide, and its full front porch sported a banner: "WELCOME HOME JONATHON WOLF BRAND."

Wolf met his uncles, his aunts, more cousins. He met the redheaded vet Maria's husband Harrison, who clapped his shoulder and pumped his hand. Willow's partner Jeremiah hung nearby, and once had leaned in and said, "You made my Willow so happy, Wolf. You got me as a friend for life, you hear?"

"Family," Willow said. "That's better than a friend."

"Brother-in-law, no less," Jeremiah said.

There were so many of them that it was overwhelming. And everyone wanted to hear the story, and to hug him, and touch him, and welcome him. He noticed a lot of them hugging and loving on his mother and father, too. He'd given Cilla's diaries to

Taylor to read. Willow thought it would ease their mother's mind to fill in those missing years, to know what her son's life had been like.

Garrett Brand, who Wolf now knew was the sheriff who'd been looking for him, and was also his uncle, rose, raised his glass of sweet tea, and tapped it with a spoon. Everyone quieted. There were tables and tables of people, and Wolf wondered how he'd ever get to know them all as every eye turned toward the big sheriff.

"I gotta tell you something, folks. This family is blessed. We've had miracles before, and plenty of 'em." He made eye contact with specific members of the clan as a murmur of agreement made the rounds. "But getting Johnny Wolf back—" He glanced at Wolf. "That's what we called you those two precious weeks we had you—Johnny Wolf. That okay with you, nephew?"

Wolf nodded solemnly. "Sure. I mean, I've grown kinda fond of Wolf, but—"

"And I've gotten fond of Ethan," said the one they called Bubba half the time.

"And I prefer Harrison to Harry," Maria's husband called out. "If anyone forgot."

Garrett shrugged. "So good luck with that, Johnny Wolf. Meanwhile, I just want to say—"

"Ahhhhhhhhhhhh!" screamed a high-pitched female voice. "Omygosh, what's happening?"

The cry had come from Lily. It was easy to remember which one she was. Her hair was paler and finer than Drew's, she was married to Ethan, and she was very, *very* pregnant.

Wait a minute…

She was rising from her chair with help from Ethan, who stood behind her. She had one hand on her back, one on her front. She was wearing a sundress and standing in a puddle of water. Oh, wait, that wasn't water.

"Ooooohhhhhh, it's for real this time," she squeaked.

Uncle Garrett, still standing, said, "I'm about to become a grandpa! Hot damn!"

Drew turned to Maria. "What do we do? What do we *do*?"

"I don't know what we do! This is the first baby of our generation," Maria cried, and she looked at her cousins. "What do we do?"

"We go to the hospital," Willow said. "That's what we do. That's what they did." She nodded to their parents. "So that's what we do." Willow clasped Wolf's arm as she hurried past him and gave a squeeze. "You won't be the newest Brand for long, brother."

He looked at Camellia and squeezed her hand as they and every other Brand on the premises headed for their vehicles and took off, a caravan of a kind.

"When things calm down," Camellia said as she walked beside him to his truck, "we need to go back to Big Bend. Now you have a last name to write in that book."

"I do, don't I?"

"You sure do."

"Do you like it?" They'd made it to his pickup. She got in her side and he got in his.

"Do I like what?"

"The name?"

She looked at him wide-eyed.

As he grinned at her and started driving she said, "I don't know. Some handsome guy once told me Camellia Rio's almost too pretty to be real."

"We could hyphenate," Wolf said. "Become the Rio-Brands."

"The Rio-Brands from the Rio Grande?" she asked, laughing softly, like she thought he was kidding around with her.

The other vehicles had all sped out of the long driveway and underneath the Texas Brand arch, but Wolf pulled the truck over right underneath it. Then he reached past her to open the glove compartment.

"The nurses gave me Mom's things when she passed. I put them in here and kind of forget about them till I was going through 'em early this morning." He pulled out a small box and Camellia sucked in a breath.

He opened it, revealing a perfect diamond ring. "It was Grandma Sage's. Ma wore it every day since she passed. Now I'd like you to wear it."

"Wolf," she whispered.

"I know what's between us is new, Camellia, but I also know… it's *you*. It's *you*, you know?"

"I know it's you, too," she said.

"Yeah?"

"Yeah," she said, nodding, and he leaned in and kissed her while sliding the ring onto her finger.

When he raised his head again, Camellia laughed softly.

"What's so funny?" he asked.

She threaded her fingers through his hair. "When I was little, I used to worry all the time that I'd never get to have a big wedding, because I had such a small family."

Then she laughed some more, and Wolf started laughing, too, as he put his truck into gear and aimed them toward El Paso.

They pulled away, leaving a cloud of love-infused dust beneath the arch above the Texas Brand.

ALSO BY MAGGIE SHAYNE

SMALL-TOWN CONTEMPORARY SERIES

The Texas Brand

The Oklahoma Brands

The McIntyre Men

The Texas Brand: Generations

THRILLERS & ROMANTIC SUSPENSE SERIES

Brown and de Luca Return

The Fatal series

Shattered Sisters

Danger After Dawn

PARANORMAL ROMANCE

The Portal

Wings in the Night

The Immortals

By Magic

ABOUT THE AUTHOR

New York Times and *USA Today* bestselling novelist Maggie Shayne has published 112 novels and novellas for numerous major publishers. She also spent a year writing for American daytime TV dramas *The Guiding Light* and *As the World Turns*. But her heart was in her books, and she'd found it impossible to do both.

Now, she is excited to be publishing with dream-publisher, Oliver Heber Books and she's having more fun than ever.

Maggie lives in a century-and-a-half old farmhouse with two waterfalls outside, in the rural hills of Cortland County NY with her husband Lance, who builds waterfalls for a living, and their dogs. There are always, always dogs.

A small press bound by the belief that every voice matters.

Sign up for our newsletter to learn about new releases and more.

Buy directly from us to save on ebooks, book bundles, and special editions.

Follow us on social media:

facebook.com/oliverheberbooks
instagram.com/oliverheberbooks
tiktok.com/@oliverheberbooks
bsky.app/profile/oliverheberbooks.bsky.social
youtube.com/@OliverHeberBooksPublisher
oliverheberbooks.substack.com
amazon.com/oliverheberbooks